Henry Clay Price

How to Make Pictures

Easy Lessons for the amateur Photographer

Henry Clay Price

How to Make Pictures
Easy Lessons for the amateur Photographer

ISBN/EAN: 9783337388362

Printed in Europe, USA, Canada, Australia, Japan

Cover: Foto ©Andreas Hilbeck / pixelio.de

More available books at **www.hansebooks.com**

HOW TO MAKE PICTURES:

EASY LESSONS

FOR THE

AMATEUR PHOTOGRAPHER.

BY

HENRY CLAY PRICE.

Revised Edition.

NEW YORK:
SCOVILL MANUFACTURING COMPANY.
W. IRVING ADAMS, AGENT.
1882.

PREFACE.

In the space of eight weeks a second edition of this book has been demanded. This must be due to the awakening of a great popular desire for amateur photography. The devotees are to be found among scientists, microscopists, bankers, merchants, the ladies, the youth, yachtsmen, canoeists; in fact it would be hard to say where they are not, and it is because of a love of the art, the increase of adherents, and the great success which has attended their efforts, that the author finds cause for congratulation.

"There is a pleasure in the pathless woods,
There is a rapture on the lonely shore,
There is society where none intrudes,
By the deep sea, and music in its roar;
I love not man the less, but nature more,
From these our interviews, in which I steal
From all I may be, or have been before,
To mingle with the universe, and feel
What I can ne'er express, yet cannot all conceal."

INTRODUCTORY CHAPTER.

"SEEMS!—nay is." This was the compliment paid to stereoscopic pictures when they were first made, so realistic did they seem. From the dim outline, the faint image discovered by Daguerre, photography has risen to be an art. Instead of unreal likenesses, portraits can now be made which *speak* through the perfectly reproduced expression of the face, and the sentiment indicated by the pose. Marvelously, too, are the beauties and glories of nature mirrored.

The latest and most rapid advance in the art is due to the discovery of the sensitiveness of a gelatine film. This knowledge has been practically applied in the introduction of plates prepared with such a coating. These are called " dry plates," to distinguish them from plates which must pass through the silver bath and be used while wet.

Gelatine plates are now in general use for taking pictures of outdoor scenes, such as landscapes, houses, groups of people, and all animated subjects.

The rapidity with which an exposure can be made is a very great recommendation in their favor wherever these plates are used. Vessels under full sail, horses speeding around a race-course, and even trains under full headway, have been depicted by the gelatine film, as though all motion were instantly suspended.

To the amateur the dark tent, with its hidden, mysterious manipulations, was forbidding. It is no longer necessary for him to be encumbered with it. The poisonous chemicals of the old process, which soiled the dress and stained the fingers, were odious. These, and the dusty, burdensome camera, can be put with the relics of the "deacon's one-hoss shay."

An equipment consisting of a tripod, lens, and camera, dry plates and holders, are all that need now be carried by the view taker, weighing so little as not to be counted burdensome to any one. Naturally, amateur photography has been given a wonderful impetus by these improvements, which make it a pleasant accomplishment; and its scope and mission are well worthy of consideration.

As a recreation, compare practice with a camera and the search for good picture subjects to archery, rowing, lawn tennis, and other sports. Is it not as pleasant, profitable, and cultivating? To saunter through green fields or by the river side with the eye alert for picturesque panoramas, to select what is worthy to be produced and treasured, ever comparing, criticising, and admiring, will be found to be no mean diversion, and will educate any one to look with keener eye and greater zest for the beautiful in nature. The exercise I commend is exhilarating, and there will not be the danger from over-exertion to be found in some sports. Besides the giving of health, there are studies made, perhaps unconsciously, adventures sure to be met with, and the results of the sport to bring home. Our country presents scenes of as great beauty as any other, with the diversity that all can offer. Torrid, temperate, or frigid; plains, hills, and mountains—all are ours. There is scope enough for the amateur.

As an aid to the work of the artist, the camera has already been promoted by some who have won national fame as landscape painters. Do they disdain the methods of the "old masters" in their art? Not by any means. This is a time for progression, and art will not sulk and frown upon an innovation that helps out in its tasks and gives a standard to judge the correctness of outline, perspective, and shading.

The camera, in adding to the number of pictures an artist can produce, will not detract from the merit of the productions. The artist's model poses for him as a pattern of loveliness to be glorified in his ideal. The lines of beauty are not a lesson of a day: many times must the study be repeated. Rare is the memory that can disdain all helps; and therefore I commend to the artist a portfolio, containing not alone crude sketches with colors faultily limned, but also with photographic productions, such as landscapes, groups of animated objects, marine views, as the fancy inclines. Combining relaxation with the gathering of these finished suggestions, work for a whole season in the studio could in a short time be· obtained.

At the time of writing, an artist is journeying and gleaning views along the Amazon. He took with him his easel a portable photographic outfit, and when he returns it will be with a satchel packed with reminders of tropical luxuriance of verdure to be transferred to canvas. If the novice and the baffled student of art find it hard to delineate nature, or to make their fancies real, let them be wise and compare their pictures with those made by the servitor camera. By its use copies of the rare paintings of the old world can be made and brought home to be companions of the studio.

The teaching of object drawing could well be supplemented by days in the field with this docile instrument, and as the result botanical specimens would receive better representation on paper, and more appreciation. There are many who are connoisseurs of art: artists they would be, but cannot, as not even the pencil will do their bidding. Commend to them the camera, which will treasure what they longed to be able to represent.

Poor is the traveler in foreign lands who does not return with mementoes for himself and those he loves, in part to prove what he saw, and also to keep the scenes alive in memory. What more fitting, and what can tell the story like a collection of views! No power of description can equal them.

Within the memory of the young how much has been added to the adornment of home! In greater part this is due to the laudable efforts and design of the ladies. This improvement is noticeable in the dwellings of nearly all, whether of high or low degree. Now that a photographic outfit can be so easily carried about, and pictures so readily made by the gentler sex, this means of aiding decorative work will be sure to be used by them. Cheap prints and crude crayon work must be put away in garrets and be superseded by photographed views, scenes of the old hillside homestead, pictures made in distant countries, or reminders of the summer holidays. Set in tasteful frames adorning the walls, or bound between covers, the claim to ownership would be a double one, that of creation and possession. Oil paintings of rare merit would not be supplanted. There is room for both.

Does a student want for satisfying pleasure? Let him try the camera. It will aid him in the practical researches of botany, entomology, mineralogy, and—what not?—and also prepare him, by the stimulation of exercise, for the better study of each. By representations of the specimens captured, he can compare results with his instructors, or men more learned than himself. A scholar's time will not be thrown away if he in this manner courts only health.

The explorer overcomes obstacles of travel to give the result of his discoveries to others; but how can he make it real to them in a story or lecture? It is a simple task if he has returned with pictures of what he has seen. These may be bound in his books. How much better Bayard Taylor's works would be could he thus have illustrated them! Or the same pictures can be transferred to magic lantern slides and thrown on to a white screen, holding the keen attention of an audience.

A missionary in the center of China is now supplementing his report to the home secretary by scenes reproduced from his daily experience among the pagans, showing their wretched condition serving heathen deities, and the awakened desire for a refinement of living as the result of the Gospel's mission. Pages of description will not tell as much as a few of such pictures. To the exile for Christianity's sake, the use of an amateur viewing outfit will be a welcome addition to the privileges he enjoys.

The farmer can find use for the camera to display the progress of cultivation in his fields. It will not be an expensive luxury; and why should his life be all work and no play? I think he will find greater satisfaction if he can look up from his toil long enough to analyze that which surrounds him and rewards his efforts.

Utility is in the spirit of the times, and our friend, the camera, would join with it. The practical part it is destined to play is now beginning to be foreseen.

To-day the best magazines and weeklies have this instrument as their "artist on the spot." Faithful and good illustrations will be the result for the future, beside which some of the old productions of imagination will hide in shame. Correspondents for papers, or in mercantile business, may, at times, find a pocket camera almost invaluable to give a finish to descriptions.

Government surveys and all topographical records are now more complete because our modest friend has noiselessly performed its part.

The wares of the merchant or manufacturer can henceforth be better and more cheaply illustrated in catalogues and price lists. In order not to be outdone, the example of some of the leading representatives of these branches of industry must be followed. *This is not chimerical!* The camera is now assigned to regular duty midst the din of toil — this silent worker!

To show a house, a bit of real estate, cattle, horses, or a pile of logs; a piece of mechanism or machinery; any new design of furniture, hangings, carpets, or ten thousand other objects, by a picture representation, when other methods would be quite expensive or unavailable, is a happy subterfuge.

Architects, with a neatly arranged collection of exteriors and interiors, are the more inspired. Their patrons would be aided in selection by a more extensive number than they usually have, especially by pictures showing more of detail in the separate parts that make up dwellings. In the drawing up of their specifications, or, in fact, in those drawn up by any craft or profession, ample illustrations would make the language used more explicit with less verbiage.

It is a wise rule adopted by insurance companies, to ascertain not only the nature of the goods on which the risk is to be assumed, but also that of the surroundings. One man hired to make such surveys of property, quick to see and apply an idea, adopted a pocket camera to verify his conclusions concerning the desirability of the risks offered. The appointed agent sent out to appraise property for a savings bank and loan association followed his example. With the trust deeds and abstracts of title are filed away his representations of real, not speculative and visionary, securities.

That recreation is more needed in this country is not denied; nay, it is preached for, and the pen is vigorously used to agitate the subject. The nation will outgrow the hurry of youth. What shall be taken up as a respite from toil? In the rationale of pleasure the camera is destined to play a sensible part, as well as an æsthetic.

These many suggestions of its service are given to lead the current of thought to its varied capacities, some of which may not have yet been dreamed of. Pictures were the symbols earliest used to express thought unuttered, and they ever have been the language universal of the world. How to make them, what purpose they can serve, and what pleasure they will afford, should be the theme of a pen most eloquent.

How to Make Pictures.

CHAPTER I.

DESCRIPTION OF APPARATUS.

It has been the fortune of the writer to instruct many pupils in the lessons of amateur photography, and all of the success that has been attained must be due to the use of simple but explicit language. In these chapters I shall try to leave nothing to be guessed at, nor any chance for doubt; but beyond the line of actual experience and knowledge I shall not venture, hence the apparatus or other parts of an outfit here described or mentioned will be such as I am familiar with through use, and known to me to be reliable—perfectly so.

In selecting such articles—having learned by experience the importance, the *necessity*, of a good equipment—I ask every amateur to purchase what is warranted by a house of known standing and veracity, and not to get what may be cheaper, but really worthless.

In taking pictures the negative is first secured. This passes through the various stages of development, and then the prints are made, which are mounted upon card-board to suit the taste. The first operation—that of producing the negative—is all that need be done at once. The other operations are subject to the pleasure and convenience of the amateur. The accompanying illustration shows all that is needed to be carried about, and the comfort and ease with which it is done.

In the case are compactly stowed a lens, camera and holders, the focusing cloth, tripod top, and note book. *There may be more hidden there that does not pertain to the art.* In the other hand is grasped a tripod neatly folded up, which may be used in this shape as a helper when climbing steep ascents, or possibly as a means of defense from obtrusive dogs in wayside orchards.

By way of contrast with the careless, easy attitude of the figure just shown, I present one of the old veterans, who toiled along, heavily laden, to practice his beloved art. If seen now with his old-time luggage, it would be averred that he had been detained by a twenty years' sleep with Hendrick Hudson's crew.

A Good Apparatus Outfit.— Less than a year ago it was announced that a good outfit, every article of it warranted, consisting of a camera, with accompanying double dry plate holder, for making pictures 4 x 5 inches, a single achromatic lens, a carrying case in which to stow away and transport the camera, plate holders and lens, and a tripod, would henceforth be sold for $10.00.

The price astonished every one, photographers especially, although the outfits of this kind were designed particularly for the use of amateurs.

"Think," said they, "of procuring a serviceable lens alone for that sum."

Worthless toys have been offered for a trifle, which will not take a picture; but all these lenses are guaranteed. Since the introduction of the cheap outfits, I have seen, in the busy city of Waterbury, pile upon pile of lens tubes bearing the name "Waterbury" as a brand, every one of them nickel-plated and perfect in finish. When brought into use and tested by experts, these lenses have proved to be possessed of something more than beauty. Not one of the Waterbury lenses has ever been sent back to the maker as falling short of what it is guaranteed to do, and therefore I give this part of the outfit particular mention.

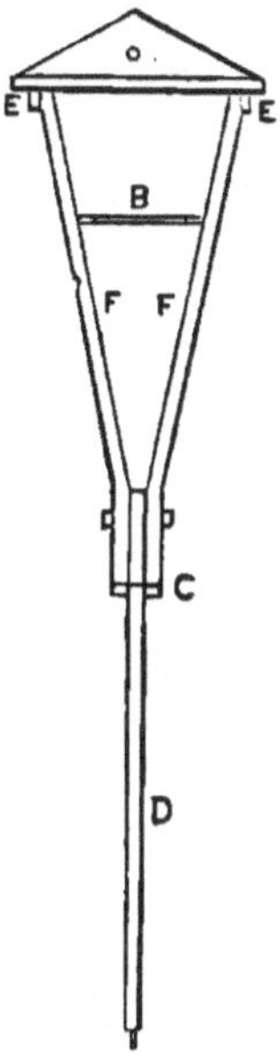

Naturally, when one has discovered the object or chosen the scene that he is desirous of photographing, the carrying case is set down, and then follows the undoing and setting up of the tripod on which the camera is to be placed and fastened. Figure 1 represents the top and one of the three legs of a common tripod. First, the part *D* of each is undoubled as far as the

FIG. 1.

brass band *C* will allow, and the button on the leg is turned, which makes it straight and rigid. The two upper of the three sticks forming a leg have holes on the outer side which slide on to the pins in the ears *E E*, belonging to the tripod top; and by pushing the loose end of the brace *B* into the slot in the opposite stick, the two pieces are sprung apart and held on to the pins.

Remember to have the brass piece *C* on the leg face out. In like manner put up the other two legs, and catch them on to the top. When set up the tripod will appear as shown in figure 2.

FIG. 2.

Figure 3 shows a camera and

lens. When not in use the tripod screw *H* is kept, as pictured here, screwed into the bed. Take it off, set the camera on the tripod top, pass the screw up through the hole in the tripod top, and screw it into the brass plate on the *under* side of the camera. A few turns of the screw will bind the camera fast to the tripod. Release the hook *B*, holding the ground-glass frame, and if the lens is in the body of the camera, take it

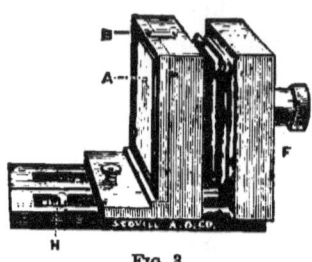

FIG. 3.

out—or out of the carrying case if stowed there—and screw it into the flange on the front of the camera as shown at *F*.

Cameras like the one shown in figure 3 are at present made in two sizes, viz.—for taking pictures 4 x 5 and 5 x 8 inches in dimensions. The material of which they are constructed is white wood, and the exteriors are stained either black or else in imitation of mahogany.

In every respect these cameras are neat, good and service-able. So it is with the rest of the outfit. The jury at the American Institute examined them in connection with the more showy apparatus, and their award of excellence covers both grades. (Extract from the judge's report at the Institute concerning the apparatus just described: "*Nothing superior to it can be found anywhere. For the attention given to outfits for amateurs, their benefit to the young, especially in the direction of encouraging art studies and a better apprecia-tion of nature's beauties; for this, as well as the whole exhibit, we recommend that a medal of superiority be awarded,*" etc., etc.)

Many an amateur makes a beginning with one of the cheap outfits, and, having achieved success, chooses something finer and higher priced.

Some there are who have but little time for recreation, and they will not care to expend more than a small sum; but amateur photography is a luring art, and the desire is easily awakened for the gems of the camera maker's skill. A feel-ing of pride concerning the equipment used, and emulation

similar to that which has led to the construction of superbly
finished yachts, is sure to be aroused among the patrons of
culture, leisure, or wealth. Such tastes and fancies may be
gratified.

Description of the Finest Apparatus.—The wise
maxim, always get the best, certainly applies to cameras. At
the outset they cost more, but less in the end, because the best
satisfies.

Spanish mahogany, finished in French polish, is used in
their construction. This wood is chosen as it wears well, and
chiefly because it will resist the effects of moisture longer than
any other. A camera that has not the property of resistance
to dampness, cannot be depended upon while passing from one
climate to another. The camera made of common wood in a
moist region swells, and its movements become clogged, and
do not work well; while in a dry, warm country the wood
contracts, and seams open, through which light penetrates,
working its baneful effect on a gelatine plate. The result is
what is commonly called " fogging," a term which will be duly
defined.

I will suppose the amateur to have purchased a superb first
quality outfit, and feel sure that he will not be disappointed in
it. The camera forming part of it is provided with a front
board that can be moved up or down, for the purpose of regu-
lating the amount of sky and foreground taken in the picture.
One of the two front boards buttoning on to the 5 x 8 size
camera has a lens screwed to the flange on its face, which
combination is used when a picture the full size of the ground
glass is desired. This front may be shifted by a lateral movement, which is of service when the box is clamped by its side
to the tripod, and an upright picture is to be made, as of
church spires or tall towers.

The second front board has on its finished side two flanges,
upon which are screwed a pair of matched lenses, to be brought
into use when stereoscopic pictures are taken ; a diaphragm or
divider is set up so that two pictures of equal size will be
made on a 5 x 8 gelatine plate.

A feature of the best cameras is that the backs are made to tilt out from the top, as shown by figure 4.

This is known in photographic parlance as a "swing back." The set screw is turned down upon the brass guide on top of the camera to regulate the incline of the back. Still another feature worthy of notice is, that the ground glass frame is hinged at the bottom, so that, instead of taking it off when the plate holder is in use, the catch at the top is drawn aside, and the frame is swung down on to the bed of the camera, as illustrated by figure 5.

Fig. 4.

Hinges are also put on the bed, allowing it to be doubled over against the back of the camera when the latter is to be packed. In focusing the brass guides on the bed keep the back and front of the camera parallel to each other; when the back is drawn out far enough, a turn of the patent cam fastens it. Such cameras as I have just described are made in three sizes, viz., for plates 4 x 5, 5 x 8, and 6½ x 8½ inches.

Fig. 5.

Neat and durable canvas-covered satchels, with telescopic covers, accompany the finest outfits. In them are carried the camera, lens or lenses, dry plate holders, focusing cloth, focusing glass, and tripod top.

Leather handles are attached to these carrying cases, but a shoulder strap can be fastened to them, and they may be carried at the side of the amateur after the fashion set by English tourists. One of these canvas cases, containing a 4 x 5 camera and one double holder, is eight inches long, the same height, and five and one-half inches broad. The weight of all is but three and one-half pounds. A 5 x 8 camera, double holder, and canvas case, together weigh five and three-quarter pounds, and the case measures eight and one-half inches long, eight and three-quarter inches high, and six inches broad.

Last, but not least, of the unsurpassed outfits, I mention the tripod, which is of the English pattern; figure 6 shows it set up.

It is firm when in position, and compact when folded up, and none has ever been made to excel it in these properties.

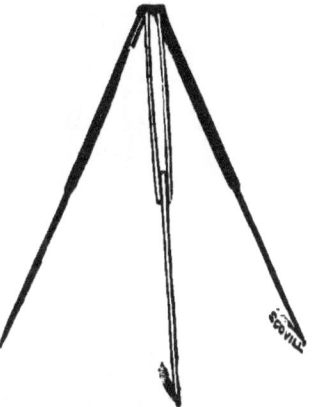

Fig. 6.

Its three legs of maple are composed of three pieces each, hinged together. To set it up, unfold the two outside pieces of a leg, bending them back toward each other until the two dowel pins in the third piece fit into the two holes in the outer joints. Of course, this is repeated with each leg. Then press together the two nearly parallel pieces, and hold the brass top (which is usually packed inside of the carrying case) flat side up, so that two of its pins will enter the holes or sockets on the outer side of the joints; release the pressure, and you will find the leg fastened to the top. Thus, also, arrange the two remaining legs, and the tripod is ready for its burden, *provided you have the flat surface of the brass top uppermost.*

Fasten the tripod and camera together by the tripod screw, passing it through the hole in the tripod top up into the plate in the bottom of the camera bed. Figure 7 shows their appearance; while beneath, as a contrast, are seen the folded tripod and the box containing the balance of the outfit.

With these cameras various lenses are used to suit the tastes and requirements of different amateurs. The one most generally selected is the rapid group lens, as it fills the following requirements: The taking of groups out of doors, general landscape work, and making instantaneous exposures.

The following cut and description will convey some idea of the means used for securing instantaneous exposures with this lens.

The drop adopted for the rapid group lens consists of a thin

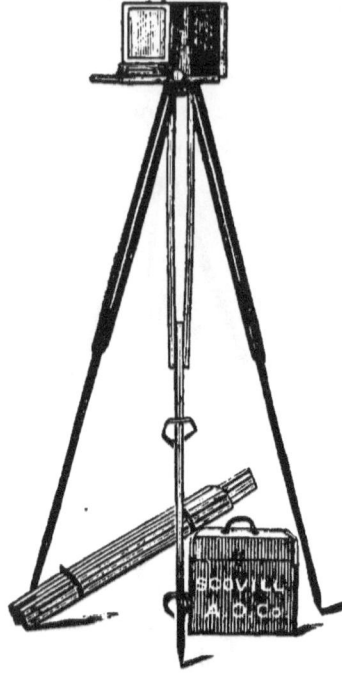

Fig. 7.

strip of brass, about three times the diameter of the lens in length, and wide enough to prevent light passing through the tube.

The piece of brass *A* has a square hole cut in its center, about equal to the diameter of the largest aperture of the tube, leaving a plain surface both above and below the hole, the lower portion shutting off the light before exposing, and the upper after exposure.

In the barrel or tube *C* a slot is cut (just behind the stop opening), both on top and underneath the tube; through this slot the above described drop will readily fall, being prevented from passing entirely through by a small knob *F* placed at the upper end.

On the under side of the tube a button *D* is placed, by which the drop is held in position (the bottom of drop resting on the same), the lower portion of the drop stopping off the light; the part with the square hole, and the upper blank portion, projecting above the tube. When this button is thrown to one side, the drop is released, and it will naturally fall by gravitation, and an exposure occurs equal to the time it would take the length of the hole in the drop to pass

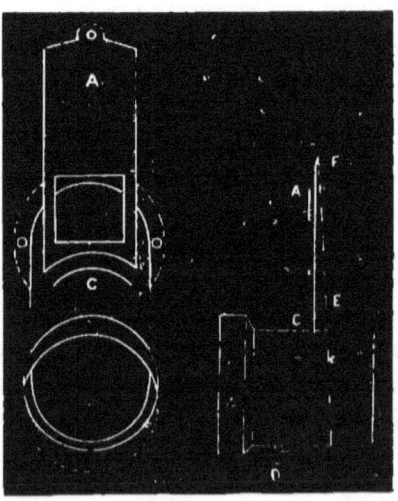

FIG 8.

the opening in the lens. The upper portion of the drop falling shuts off the light. If the exposure is required to be still more rapid, a rubber band E, placed around the tube and stretched up and over the knob F on top of the drop. or a weight attached to the eye at the bottom of the drop will accelerate its action and shorten the exposure. If you wish to copy a painting, engraving, or lettering, this lens will meet the requirements.

For landscape and stereo work I recommend the use of the American make of the wide-angle view lenses, shown by figure 9. These favorite lenses are perfectly *achromatic*, and absolutely *rectilinear ;* they embrace an angle of fully one hundred degrees, and are the most rapid wide-angle lenses made.

They are supplied with revolving diaphragms, the openings of which are adapted to the focal length of their respective lenses. Where only a limited field is required, the full aperture may be used, while with the stops of smaller diameter perfect definition is obtained to the margin of the plate. In selecting lenses of this description, the shorter focused lenses are especially adapted for street and other views in confined situations.

FIG. 9.

For general purposes a pair of five inch back focus will be found most useful to the amateur, and especially so if he intends to take stereoscopic pictures. To aid amateurs in the selection of these view lenses, I append the following table, showing the height of image produced on the focusing glass, with a few sizes, by an object twenty-five feet high, at a distance of fifty feet.

Focal Length of Lens.	Height of Image produced on Ground Glass.
$2\frac{1}{4}$ inches.	$1\frac{1}{2}$ inches.
3 "	$1\frac{3}{4}$ "
4 "	$2\frac{3}{8}$ "
5 "	3 "
6 "	$3\frac{1}{2}$ "

CHAPTER II.

Before starting out to take pictures, the plate holders must be filled with gelatine plates. Some of them hold two, and hence, if but two views are to be taken before the return, it will be best to fill but a single holder. If the amateur thinks to secure more than two picture impressions, he must govern himself accordingly in putting sensitive plates into the holders. As it is essential that this operation of filling the holders should be done in a room or closet where all other than ruby light is excluded, bear this fact in mind before leaving your base of supplies. It frequently occurs that an amateur is gone from home for a considerable length of time, and has, while away, no chance of darkening a room sufficiently in which to develop the exposed plates, or to refill his holders. In this case he must provide himself before starting with a number of holders filled with gelatine plates.

The exclusion of *white light* from the room in which the plates are either placed in the holder, or afterward developed, should be both *emphasized* and *italicised*. After you have closed the door and believe the room to be dark, do not rest satisfied; stuff the chinks and crannies. Overhead, underneath, everywhere, stop out white light. Look through the keyhole! there may not be a reporter outside, but there is as great an inquisitor who must be barred out, and it can be done effectually. Having faithfully attended to the imperative duty of securing black darkness, welcome the light which will not injure the sensitive film on the plates. This can be admitted from without by light shining through a pane of ruby glass, or ruby paper over white glass; but the more common and preferable light is that which is diffused from one of the ruby lanterns designed especially for this purpose

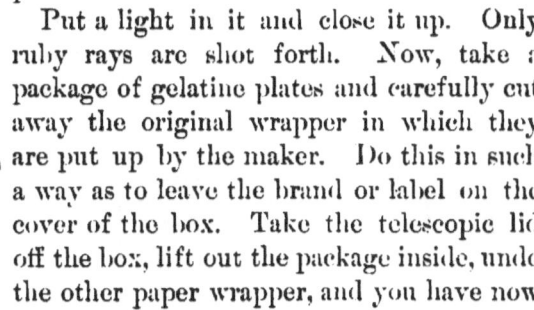

(see figure 10), and I will suppose you are provided with one.*

Put a light in it and close it up. Only ruby rays are shot forth. Now, take a package of gelatine plates and carefully cut away the original wrapper in which they are put up by the maker. Do this in such a way as to leave the brand or label on the cover of the box. Take the telescopic lid off the box, lift out the package inside, undo the other paper wrapper, and you have now come to the glass plates, with one side sensitized, which were packed with tissue paper between them.

FIG. 10.

Take out a plate, handling it as shown in figure 11, which is the proper way, and dust off its glossy sensitive surface very gently with a camel's-hair brush. This is done to guard against the possibility of any speck or particle of dust being on its surface, the presence of which would eventually make a spot or defect in the finished picture. It would not be amiss to dust off both sides of the plate.

If you cannot detect the surface having the coating of gelatine otherwise, hold the plate between you and the ruby lantern, and you will then perceive which side has been coated. Be careful to keep everything but the

FIG. 11.

camel's-hair brush away from the surface of the gelatine plate.

Take up, with the left hand, one of the double plate holders, A, pictured by figure 12, and pull out the slide C, laying it to one side. In one of the outer grooves of the holder place a

---

* Another dry plate lantern has just been introduced, more expensive than the one here illustrated, but with far greater illuminating power. Without question, it is the best one made for home purposes, but it is less portable than the other.

gelatine plate, with its sensitive side facing out. Figure 13 represents the end of a holder, and the shaded portion depicts the sensitive plate, while the dark lines denote the position of the sensitive surface during the time it is going to the scene of action, when it is exposed to white light to receive the image, and while it returns trophy-laden to the place where the victory is to be commemorated. That is anticipating, just as the amateur will be wont to do.

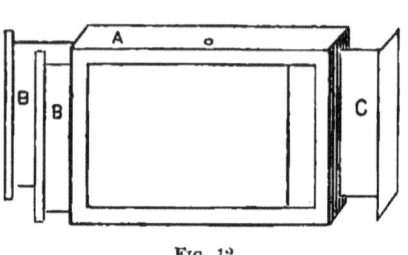

FIG. 12.   FIG. 13.

Take up another gelatine plate, or rather, handle it now like an expert, and place it in the remaining unfilled outside groove of the holder. Be sure to have the sensitive side face outward. Insert the slide *C* in the central groove of the holder, as indicated in figure 12, and push it clear in to the stopper. If the springs on this piece catch on the edges of the plates, bring a slight pressure to bear on them with the thumb and forefinger of the left hand, which will remove the trouble and permit the slide to be forced in to its hilt or so-called "stopper."

See if the slides *B B* (thus denoted in figure 12) are pushed in also. The purpose of the slide *C* is to keep light from passing through from one plate to the other during the time the first plate is going through the operation commonly called "taking the picture." Fogging is thus again avoided.

Back to back the plates are placed, and each has its own time appointed for seeing the light and treasuring what is seen. Another mission of the slide *C* is to keep the plates in focus by means of the springs on its surface. When all of the slides are pushed in as far as they were designed to go, the holder should be absolutely light-tight. It should not only be so when it is sold, but it ought to remain so, and "there's the rub" with a cheap holder. A good holder is a prime factor of an outfit of sterling worth. Better have none at all than a poor one.

But to recur, the slide C should only be taken out in order to remove the gelatine plates ready for development, or to place fresh ones in the holder, and the slides B B only drawn out during an exposure.

There is a screw or pin you will observe on the upper side of the holder. By its side is stamped the figure 1. Invert the holder and in the same position behold the figure 2. Remember about these figures when you have the plate holder in use. Give number 2 a chance to see the light. Number 1 will overdo and be spoiled if used twice.

After filling the plate holder or, if you so choose, several of them, rewrap the remaining gelatine plates of the undone package, put them in the card-board box, replace the cover, and hide away the plates from their arch enemy, *white light*, so great a blessing elsewhere. It is time to come out of seclusion, so throw open the door and put out the lantern light. There are worlds you are sighing to conquer. Away! be back to them, and study what each horizon bounds. Learn like the photographer in his study of physiognomy, that there is nothing duplicated under the sun.

CHAPTER III.

WITH the position chosen from which to take the picture—this, by the way, should be selected so that the sunlight will shine from the rear, or at one side of the camera, never in front—you set up the camera and tripod, and in doing this be sure that the top of the camera is level.

Govern yourself accordingly when spreading out or adjusting the legs of the tripod to lower the camera.

If you cannot with your eye determine about the true position of the camera, it would be well to carry with you a spirit level of vest pocket size. There are times when the camera may be pointed at a small angle upward or downward from the plane of the horizon as a variation from the rule just given, to offset which swing the ground glass to a vertical position.

Let me emphasize the command not to have the camera incline either to one side or the other. If the upright sides of the ground glass frame lean to one side, so will the picture.

The camera may be swung round by loosening the screw which binds it to the tripod. When swung far enough, turn the thumb screw until the camera is again fastened tightly to its support.

From out of the carrying case or some other receptacle pull the focusing cloth, throw it over the top of the camera, and gather it tightly at its sides. Under the hood thus formed thrust your head.

Do not cover the lens with the cloth.

The object of the hood is to shut out light excepting that which enters through the lens and throws a reversed picture on the ground glass, which acts like a semi-transparent mirror.

Uncap the lens and draw the back of the camera toward you. After a moment your eyes will become accustomed to the situation, and the picture will seem to have already been secured. It is not a permanent impression, but like that of the mirror. Continue to draw the back of the camera toward you, and the image will appear more distinctly on the ground glass. If you pull out the back too far, reverse the movement just as you are compelled to do with a pair of opera glasses. When you see the image most clearly you have obtained the right *focus ;* neither the word nor the operation is difficult; a little practice will master both. While standing in the same position look all around the edges of the ground glass, and make sure that the picture is as clearly defined there as it should be. Photographers would speak of securing "good definition."

Having made sure of this, fasten the back of the camera by a turn of the clamp screw. Now lay aside the focusing cloth where it will be safe.

Spring back the catch *B*, shown in figure 3, and put the ground glass and frame out of the way. Be careful not to break the former. Place the cap on the lens. Take a double dry plate holder, and turn it so that the heads of the dark slides face to the right (see *CC*, figure 14, showing holder in

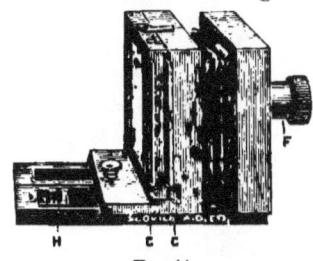

proper position). Set the holder down, and over the pins projecting from the bed of the camera, and push it gently forward until the hook from the camera catches on to the top screw.

Fig. 14.

Look now to your lens to see that the cap is still on; a knock might have brushed it off. If this were to pass unnoticed, and the dark slide *C* be drawn out, one side of the sensitive plate would necessarily catch the light before the other, with a result not at all favorable. Or, on the other hand, a longer exposure than is desirable might be given. There is a proper time to doff the cap. It is after you have pulled out the dark slide *C* nearest the camera (which please lay on top of the camera), and also after you have decided how long the sensitive plate should receive light through the lens in order to get the best results on the film.

Suppose, for illustration, your subject to be a landscape, made up of sky, trees, houses, and a pond—the atmosphere clear, and the sun brightly shining. The sky will be photographed on the film very quickly, the pond not quite as rapidly, the impression of the bright colored houses will follow next, and lastly the dark green foliage.

You have in use an achromatic lens of six inch back focus, and a stop of a quarter inch opening. (Do not be alarmed at these words, for you will or may ascertain such points about a lens when you purchase one.) The gelatine plates in use we will suppose to be what are called rapid, hence you decide upon fifteen seconds' exposure, as denoted by your watch. Uncap the lens by a quick movement, but do not jar the camera, and as soon as the allotted time has passed recap the lens, replace the watch in your pocket, and push in the dark slide. Very soon an amateur can learn to mark off seconds without having to verify the count by a timekeeper.

A little practice of counting off the flight of seconds, when there is nothing else to do, will enable you to become expert. Take out your pencil and note book, and make the following as the befitting record of observations:

No. of Holder.	No. of Plate.	Lens.	Stop.	Exposure in Seconds.	Time of Day.	REMARKS. Condition of Light, Subject, etc.
1	1	6 inch Ach.	¼	15	10 A.M.	Bright Sunlight. Berkshire Hills, Panorama.

Such notations are made by men who have had years of experience in photography. They make frequent reference to the notes, and from them deduce calculations of the length of exposure to be given under similar circumstances. Then, again, the notes enable them to compare observations with others. So, amateur friend, do not forget your note book; at least you will be driven to it to find out the numbers of the plates that have been exposed, and to thus avoid using them again.

The plate holder can now be put in the carrying case, and indeed the whole outfit be folded into its most compact form, or the tripod and camera may be carried "shoulder arms," if the amateur expects to pitch the tripod and give battle to another surrendering scene not far distant.

Ah! by way of diversity, here is a fine marine view with the blue sky, the broad expanse of the sea, boats at anchor, and a small dock to give the picture a finish. This is a treat! When you have secured the right focus, and start to substitute the plate holder in place of the ground glass, recall the fact that plate number 1 has on it a picture impression, and must not be used again; so the holder should be inverted, and figure 2 be on the uppermost side. Also remember about the dark slides facing to the right. Before uncapping the lens again, calculate how long the cap should be off.

The sky casting down direct, and the water giving back reflected light, action on the sensitive film will be more rapid than in the former view, and you therefore decide upon ten seconds' exposure. Draw out the dark slide nearest the camera. Have you got hold of the right one? 'Tis well! lay it on the camera. Uncap the lens, count ′′′′′′′′′′ (10) seconds and recap. Replace the dark slide, and return the holder, with its two hidden trophies, to the carrying case. Have your note book tell the story of the capture, and where it took place.

By this time perchance you are hungry enough to "eat a bear;" you did not think that luncheon would be needed, so little appetite did you have before starting, but now you are certain that you will go home and see that dinner is served promptly this day at least.

CHAPTER IV

DEVELOPMENT OF THE PLATE.

IT is not essential that the operation next in order with the gelatine plate shall follow at once, or the same day or week. The amateur can suit his convenience in the matter. Dry plates have been exposed in the Arctic Regions and developed in England. They have been used in Africa and brought home over six thousand miles, after months of travel, to be developed.

For the above manipulation the following list of accessories are requisite: Two vulcanite trays, one four-ounce glass graduate, a set of five-inch Japanese scales and weights; and, of chemicals, say one ounce bromide potassium, one ounce sulphuric acid c. p., one pound neutral oxalate potash, one pound protosulphate of iron, one pound hyposulphite of soda, and one pound alum.

These accessories will probably be kept where the dry plates also are stored. Into this closet or room are taken the dry plate holders containing the exposed plates, the door of the room is shut, and again all white light is barred, thrust, and stuffed out. The *seance* can now go on by ruby light.

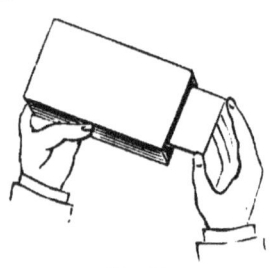

Take out the central septum (slide *C*, figure 12) from a holder, which latter please grasp with the left hand as shown in figure 15, and, holding the right hand to within an inch of the opened end, tilt forward or raise the

Fig. 15.

other end of the holder so that the gelatine plates will slide down and strike against the fingers of the right hand. Figure 15

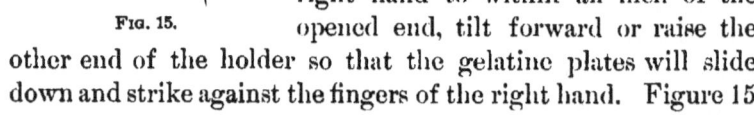

illustrates this also. The uppermost plate is taken out of the holder, being grasped by the thumb and forefinger of the right hand, as shown in figure 11, and then the holder is so inclined that the other plate will slide back into its former place.

The holder can now be set aside. Lower the gelatine plate into a vulcanite tray, and *keep the sensitive side uppermost.* *Look to this!* Put the slide *C* back into the holder. From a pitcher or glass pour clean water into the tray until it is half filled. Leave the plate in this cold water bath, and mix your developer solution as follows: With a graduated glass, in appearance like figure 16, measure out two ounces of oxalate of potash solution, which is made by the following formula:

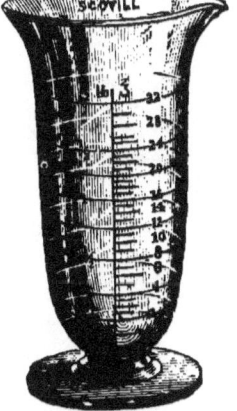

Water, twenty ounces, into which dissolve five ounces neutral oxalate potash and twenty grains of bromide of potassium.

If the solution does not turn blue litmus paper red, then add enough drops of a saturated solution of oxalic acid to make it do so. This solution will keep indefi-

FIG. 16.

nitely. Pour the solution from the graduated glass into a tumbler kept for this use. Rinse out the graduate, and pour into it one-quarter ounce protosulphate of iron solution prepared as follows:

Water, twenty ounces, with five ounces of protosulphate of iron dissolved therein. To this add twenty drops of sulphuric acid c. p.

This solution will also keep well. Pour the quarter ounce of iron solution into the two ounces of oxalate of potash. A few rotations of the tumbler will mix the two. Set the tumbler down, and pour off the water in the tray, using care that the gelatine plate does not slide out, and also that its surface is not handled. When the water has been drained off, pour the developing solution from the tumbler into the tray. Should any air bubbles form, a slight touch of the finger will displace them. Bring the ruby lantern close to the side of the pan (see figure 17), so that you may better note the action of the developer upon the gelatine film. If the

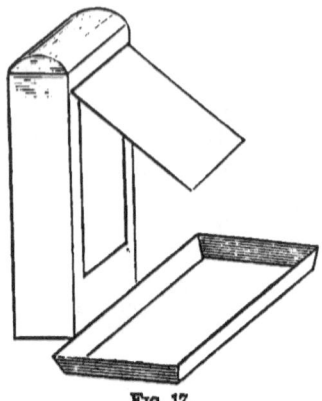

latter, after a short time, shows no sign of a change taking place, consider that you did not give the plate too long an exposure, and such being the case, flow the developer back into the tumbler, and to it add another quarter ounce of the iron solution. Shake the tumbler a few times, and pour the new solution into the tray. Watch the plate, but restrain impatience. Along its edge a dark streak appears, which indicates that the

Fig. 17.

sky is developing. Soon the outline of a building with windows, and general details appear, and lastly the foliage—such would be the order if the picture possessed these features. Allow the gelatine plate to remain in the developer until what is of a milky whiteness begins to turn gray in color, and the image seems to fade away, then pour the developer into the tumbler, and flow clean water on to the plate. Replace it with fresh, raising the plate so that the water may wash the under as well as the upper side of it; again renew with fresh water, and prepare for the next process, which is termed fixing the plate.

CHAPTER V.

POUR into the unused tray enough to half fill it of the hyposulphite of soda solution, the formula for preparing which is as follows:

Water, twenty-four ounces, with four ounces of hyposulphite of soda dissolved therein.

The finger of caution must here point to a warning: ☜ *Never use this latter tray for any other than a hyposulphite of soda solution.*

Remove the plate from the tray where it lies, handling it just as has been illustrated, and place it in the fixing solution contained in the second tray. Again be sure to have the sensitive or film side up. Keep the plate in this solution until all the milky whiteness has disappeared from the back of the plate—this will be noted by raising the plate with the finger and examining the lower side. If any white patches remain, replace the plate in the solution Patches must thus artistically be hidden from view, so allow a little additional time before taking out the plate, to be sure that they have all disappeared. Then take the plate out of the solution, and wash it thoroughly. White light will not now harm it, so it can be carried to a sink outside of the darkened room.

Every particle of hyposulphite of soda should be removed from the film and plate. The washing is done by permitting a gentle stream of water to flow over each side of the plate. Do not permit the fingers to touch the film, as thus the negative would be marred.

After carefully and completely cleansing the plate, rinse out the developing tray and pour it half full of the alum solution, which is mixed according to the formula presented here:

Water, twenty ounces, and all the alum it will take and hold in solution, or, in other words, a " saturated solution."

Place the plate, film side up, into the new bath, and permit it to remain there five minutes, while you cleanse your hands from any adhering soda solution.

Remove the plate from the tray, wash it for a few seconds, and set it up to dry, which may require a number of hours. Do not use heat to dry the plate, as you would thus melt the film, and so cause the gelatine to run about or off the plate. Then your picture would resemble "Castles in Spain," nothing more defined, everything depending on the power of imagination. I present in figure 18 a very convenient receptacle for

holding gelatine plates when drying, which is called a negative rack. Set the plate in this, or where it will not be disturbed while drying.

Plate number 2 can now be put through the course of development and fixing, and into the negative rack. Before doing this, however, that is,

FIG. 18.

handling plate number 2, empty the tray containing the alum solution back into the bottle, wash the tray out, and carry it into the dark room; also throw away the contents of the developing tumbler, which please rinse out also. If the ruby lantern has been extinguished, relight it. Once more banish all white light from the closet. Briefly permit me to enumerate what plate number 2 is to pass through. 1st, take the plate out of the holder. 2d, place it in the developing pan, and pour water on it. 3d, pour off the water, and replace it with the mixed developing solution. 4th, wash and fix the plate. 5th, wash and place the plate in the solution of alum. 6th, again wash the plate, and set it in the negative rack to dry. The presumption in this summary is that the gelatine plate was given the proper length of exposure.

Over-Exposure.—Suppose a case where too long an exposure has been given. To correct the effects of this it will be necessary to reduce the developer with water, say one ounce of water to two ounces of the oxalate solution; add to this dilution an eighth of an ounce (that is, one drachm) of the iron solution, and two or three drops of a sixty grain solution of bromide of potassium, which is made by dissolving sixty grains of bromide of potassium in one ounce of water.

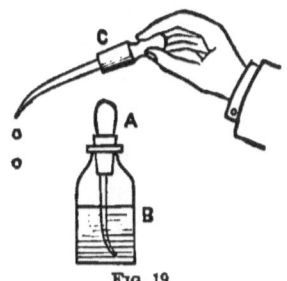

Fig. 19.

Label the bottle, *B*, containing this mixture, cut a hole in the cork, and in opening insert a dropping tube (see figure 19). The rubber cap *A* is compressed while the tube is in the bottle, forcing the air out of it. Upon taking off the pressure, the solution is drawn upward into the tube. On removing the tube and pressing the rubber cap, as shown at *C*, one or more drops may be expelled, according to requirement.

A Stock Developing Bottle.—While pursuing the subject of development, it will not be amiss to call the attention of the amateur to a very convenient receptacle illustrated by figure 20. This is a bottle with an outlet near the bottom,

Fig. 20.

which opens into the end of a rubber tube having at or near the other extremity a cork through which the rubber tube has been drawn. Into this bottle pour twenty-four ounces (one and one-half pints) of oxalate of potash solution. Pour on enough paraffin oil to cover the oxalate to the depth of half an inch. Measure out three ounces of the protosulphate of iron solution and pour it into the bottle, where it will penetrate the oil and combine with the oxalate solution, forming ferrous oxalate developer, in appearance red. After the plate has been immersed in the water, and this poured off, the tray is placed in such a position that enough of the developer in the bottle is drawn to cover the plate. This is done by removing the cork and lowering that end of the rubber tube over the tray, which permits the developer to flow into it. When the development has gone on sufficiently, remove the plate, wash it, and place it in the fixing solution. While the plate rests there, a funnel, with a filter inside, is placed with its small end in the neck of the stock bottle.

Take up the tray with the developer in it, and pour the solution into the filter lined funnel, whence it will percolate down into the stock bottle cleared of its impurities. After this, remove the funnel and cork the bottle.

With the stock bottle you may have a developing solution ready for use at any time, and the developer can be used over and over again. The oil is poured on the surface of the solution to keep air away from it, and prevent precipitation. If, after a while, the developer does not seem to act with energy, add a quarter of an ounce of the iron solution. If many plates have been developed with this solution, I should advise that to each ounce of the solution remaining two grains of bromide of potassium be added. Label this bottle " *Old Developer*," and in the same kind of a bottle mix a fresh developer as before compounded, viz., oxalate of potash, twenty-four ounces, with the oil on top, then three ounces of the iron solution. This is the one to be used next in developing your plates.

You ask, perhaps, for a method to tone up a negative that is weak, but has good detail. The manipulation should proceed in this manner: After your regular developer has brought out the detail, showing a lack in strength, pour the developer back into its bottle, then flood the plate with some of the old developer containing the extra bromide of potassium. In this way the negative will acquire strength.

From this description, chemical manipulation may seem complicated, but the processes are not really so. Rather than have the amateur grope along, trying to discover what will bring success and what will lead to error, I have endeavored to mark out each step to be taken. Still, if the amateur hesitates and wavers, not trusting his own ability to manipulate a plate, he can have the development done by a professional photographer, and also the printing, toning, and mounting of the picture. I do not recommend this. To "go it alone" is the true American way. If doubts arise, consult with some one of experience, and believe in your ability to do what other amateurs have done.

CHAPTER VI.

WE left the negative in the rack, drying, and it must be thoroughly dried before the next process is attempted. My plan is to leave the negative in the rack over night to dry. It follows next in order that a coating of varnish (prepared and sold for this purpose) should be put over the film on the nega-

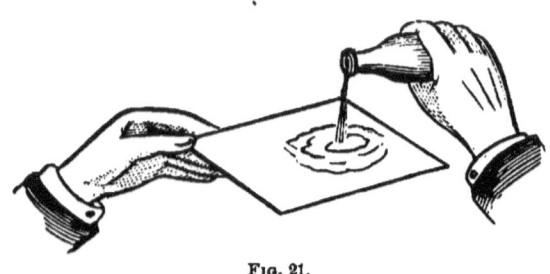

Fig. 21.

tive to preserve and protect it. So warm the plate slightly; do not use much heat; only just sufficient to give the plate an indication of warmth.

Grasp the plate by the corner with the left hand in the manner shown in figure 21. Have the film side up. With the right hand remove the cork from the bottle of varnish, and, taking it up, pour enough on the plate to make a pool, which can be spread over the surface of the plate, but not so much that the varnish will run off at the edge. Figure 21 illustrates the act of pouring out the varnish. Incline the plate so that the varnish will flow to the upper right hand corner, vary the inclination, and send the varnish to the upper left hand corner, then around to the corner held by the hand, and finally to the lower right hand corner. It will, of course, be surmised that the object of these movements is to coat the film on the plate over evenly with varnish. When the varnish has reached the lower right hand corner, the bottle should be placed as indicated by figure 22, so that it will catch the surplus varnish. Gradually the corner distant from the bottle is raised so that all

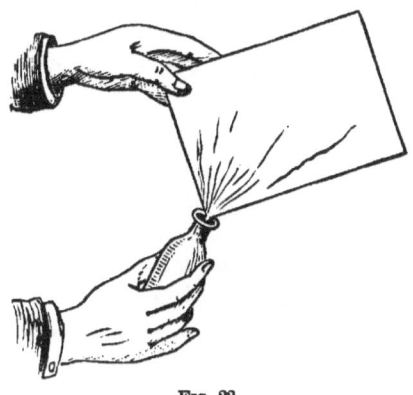

Fig. 22.

the excess of varnish will run off the plate, to accelerate which give the plate a slight rocking motion to and fro from right to left.

As soon as the varnish ceases to run off, remove the bottle, cork it, and draw the lower corner of the plate over a bit of paper to wipe off any drops clinging to the edge. Warm the

Fig. 23.

plate to dry the varnish, using only sufficient heat to cause it to dry with glossy brilliancy.

Set aside the varnished negative for a few hours to cool and harden, and then it will be ready for the printing frame. When a number of negatives have been developed and varnished, there are two methods of preserving them from the dust and from scratches. One is by putting them in envelopes made of stout paper, and called "negative preservers," which are sold to correspond to different sized negatives. Another way is by placing the negatives in boxes like the one shown in figure 23. These are called "negative boxes," and are constructed to hold twenty-four negatives, which latter are slipped into the grooves at the two sides, and thus kept from rubbing.

CHAPTER VII

In other words, producing a positive picture on paper from a negative. For this purpose are needed two porcelain trays, one printing frame, some ready sensitized paper, a bottle of chloride of gold, a quarter pound acetate of soda, one ounce chloride of lime, one pound hyposulphite of soda. This is a fair proportion of chemicals. Before commencing to print determine how many pictures you want from each negative, and cut the proper amount of sensitized paper into pieces the size of the negative. There are in each sheet sixteen pieces, four by five inches in size. Use an ivory paper cutter, and do not allow your fingers to touch the sensitive or glossy side of the paper. Put the pieces of sensitive paper in a large envelope, which please place in a shallow paper box and conceal in a dry and dark place until wanted for use. Sensitized paper should be handled only in a weak light.

Figure 24 is that of a printing frame with one half of the back-board unfastened and opened up.

Unfasten the other half and take the whole back-board out. Dust out the inside of the frame, and also dust off the negative. The outside of the frame may not be harmed by the same operation. Put the negative in the printing frame so that the film side is up, and upon it place a piece of sensitized paper, with its glossy side down. Replace the back-board in the printing frame. Note that the paper underneath is smooth. Fasten the springs by sliding the ends under the buttons on the frame, using gentle pressure to avoid breaking the glass negative underneath. The placing of the sensitized paper in the frame must be done in a subdued light. Carry the printing frame, when all closed up, to the window, lay it upon the sill, and let the light fall upon the front of the frame. Occasionally remove the frame from the window, stepping back into the room to examine the print. Loosen one of the

FIG. 24.

springs, raise one half of the back to a perpendicular position, as shown in figure 24, bend back the sensitized paper, and see how the printing is getting on. When the print looks darker than you wish the finished picture to appear, remove it from the frame and place it away from the light; a drawer or a box is a good receptacle. Put another piece of sensitized paper in the frame and continue as before, until you have secured the desired number of prints from this negative. The following cautions will not come amiss at this point. Never drop your negatives into the printing frame, but rather lower them in gently.

Some negatives may require continuously the full benefit of the sun's rays on the printing frame, but the greater number do better in a more subdued light. Never permit anything to throw a reflection on your frame while printing with it.

When examining the print, always do so in a weak light. Use care in putting in the paper, and do not scratch the negative.

CHAPTER VIII.

ALTHOUGH toning is the next operation, you will naturally prepare the toning and fixing solutions *before proceeding to make the prints.* The formula for preparing the stock toning solution is as follows:

Into seven and one-half ounces of water dissolve fifteen grains chloride of gold and sodium, then add to it three hundred grains acetate of soda and seven drops of a saturated solution of chloride of lime.

You now have a solution which should be made twenty-four hours before using. Being a stock solution it will keep, and is always ready when wanted. Pour clean water into one of the porcelain trays, and into this bath place the prints. Toning should be done in a weak light. Do not get too near a window, but have sufficient light to see distinctly without requiring guess-work. After the prints have soaked awhile in the water, pour it off and renew with fresh. This should be repeated a number of times, and at the last change permit the prints to soak while you prepare the toning bath according to the following formula:

Take of the stock toning solution one-half ounce, pour it into the unused porcelain tray, add to it seven ounces of water and agitate the tray in order to mix them well.

The water is now drained off the prints, and they are placed in the solution just mixed face downward, one at a time, pressing them down into it with the fingers. When you have finished this, commence leisurely to turn them over, and this

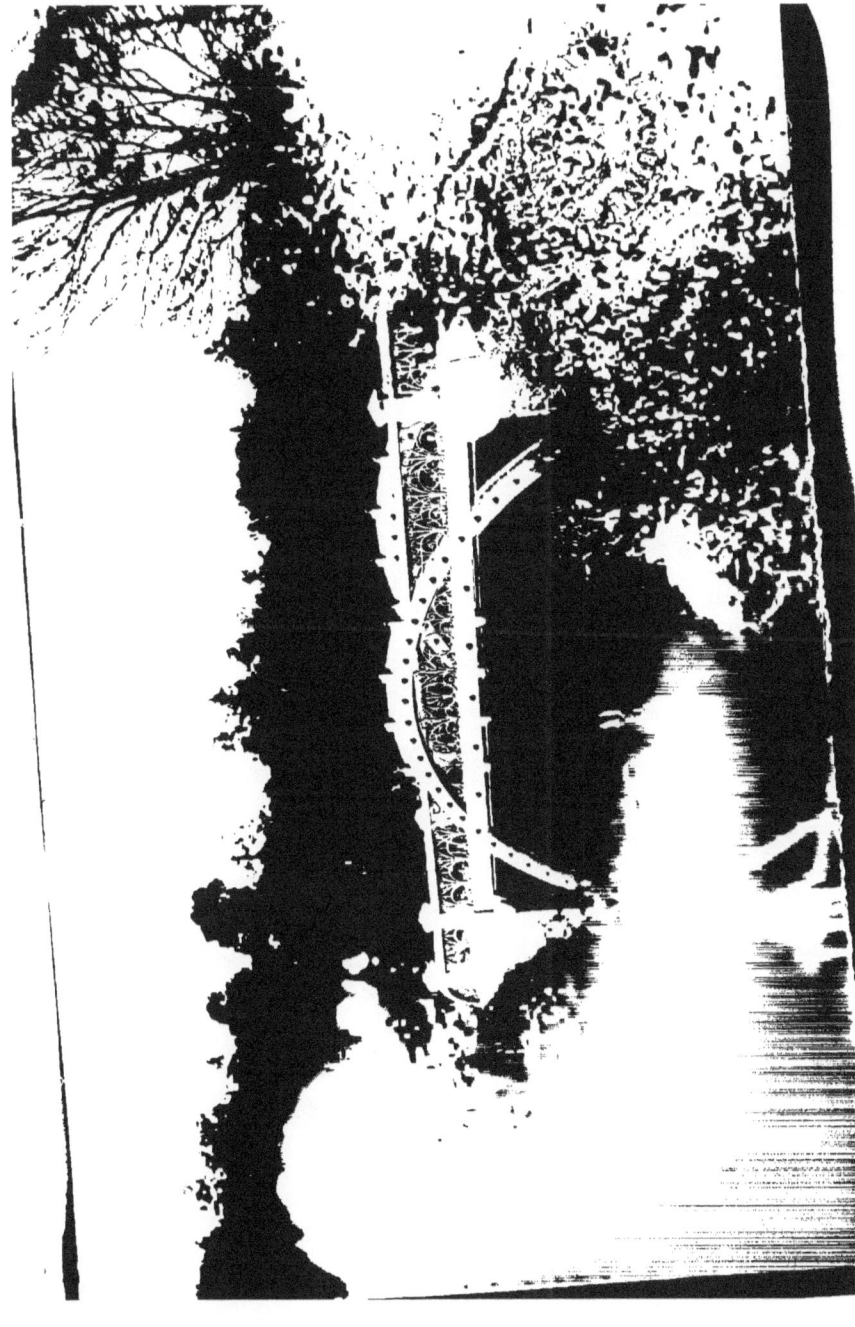

reversal or turning over should continue while they remain in this solution, in order to secure even tones. The prints are presumed to be toned sufficiently when, on examination by transmitted light, the whites are found to be clear, and by reflected light the pictures have a purple tint. Remove the prints from the toning solution (which preserve for future use) and wash them well in clear water, using the now empty dish for the purpose.

A very simple toning bath may be made with French azotate and chloride of gold and sodium. *Into seven and one-half ounces of water put seven and one-half grains chloride of gold and sodium.* Label the bottle containing the mixture *chloride of gold solution.* Combine six ounces of water with one ounce of French azotate, to which add one and one-half ounces of the chloride of gold solution. Thus the toning bath is made.

Fixing the Prints.—Pour this water off and place the prints in the fixing bath, which is thus made up:

Hyposulphite of soda four ounces, common salt one ounce, sal soda (washing soda) one-half ounce, and water thirty-two ounces.

Prepare this solution the day before it is to be used, or warm to ninety degrees. Put the prints in the fixing solution to remain twenty minutes. (This should be used but for one lot of prints.) After fixing the prints, wash them thoroughly and well, and then hang them up to dry. As stated before, it is necessary to have all trace of the hyposulphite of soda removed from the prints. This is accomplished by long washing in running water. In the photographic galleries this washing is continued all night, which would not in all cases be convenient for the amateur.

Some five years ago Mr. H. J. Newton, a well-known amateur, brought before the photographic community a simple and effectual means of removing the hyposulphite of soda from the prints with far less washing, to wit: First prepare a stock solution by dissolving two ounces of acetate of lead in sixteen ounces of water. After the prints are fixed, wash them in three or four changes of clear water, allowing them to remain in each change a short time. While in the last change measure out four quarts of water, to which add two ounces of the above lead solution. This addition will give the water a milky appearance. Add acetic acid until the solution clears up, and place the prints in this solution, leaving them there from five to ten minutes; then remove and wash in several changes of clear water, and hang them up to dry. This ended, they are ready for mounting, which can be done to suit the taste.

Blue Prints.—There is another method of producing a positive picture on paper, which is very simple. It is called the "*blue process*," and is much used for reproducing mottoes, drawings, manuscripts, etc. The manipulation is as follows: Place the negative in the printing frame, film side up; upon it lay a piece of ferro.-prussiate paper, colored side down. After fastening in the back, carry the printing frame to the window, and turn the front side out to receive the sunlight for from three to ten minutes. Occasionally take in the frame to examine the printing, and as soon as the image is distinctly seen on the paper, place the print in a pan of clear water for from fifteen to thirty minutes, or until the whites of the picture are clear, when you will have a permanent blue print on white paper. The handling of this paper should be done in a very weak light until after it is washed. Lamp or gaslight will not hurt it.

CHAPTER IX

TRIMMING AND MOUNTING PRINTS.

PRINTS can be trimmed, one at a time, by laying a ruler over them, and cutting along the straight edge with a very sharp knife; but the more scientific method is to use glass forms, as the picture can be seen  through them, and by shifting the form the best portion of the print may be selected. Lay the print on a thick light of glass, over it adjust the glass form, and with a sharp penknife cut all around the edges. Better than a knife for this purpose is one of

FIG. 25.

the straight trimmers illustrated by figure 25, as it makes a clean cut edge, not a rough or uneven one.

Mounting the Prints.—When through trimming the prints, my plan is to dampen a light of glass, at the same time making sure that it is clean. Then I take each print separately, and immerse it in water until it lies flat. (By this time you realize that prints, as well as negatives, must accept the doctrine of total immersion.) Then place it face down upon the light of glass; on top of it put another print facing down, and so continue until all of them have been dampened and thus piled up. Drain off the surplus water so that the prints will not be too wet.

The paste used for mounting must be sweet. Sour paste will spoil your prints. Do not forget this fact, and you will not, after a while, have to lament about the fading and staining of some choice view. *Parlor paste* is the best for an amateur's use, as it keeps well and is always ready for service. It is only essential to see that the bottle or jar containing it is corked (when not in use) to keep out dust. With this paste keep a bristle brush—a two inch brush is best—as a large surface can be spread over with paste in a short time, and it will do the work evenly.

After wetting the brush and squeezing out the water, dip it in the paste, and apply this to the upper surface or back of the top print on the pile, passing the brush backward and forward until an even coating is put on. See that the edges are not neglected. With a knife blade lift one corner of this print, grasp it with the finger and thumb of the left hand, and raise it off the other prints; at the same time take hold of the lower edges and turn it in such a manner that the print will be suspended paste side down between the two hands. Now bring it over to the card-board or mount, and poise it over the middle. Gently lower the center of the print down to the mount, and carefully push one edge, and then the other, down to the card-board surface. Place a clean piece of paper on the print, and, commencing at the center, rub with the hand toward one end and then toward the other, to press out all air from beneath the print. If it appears to be smoothly pasted on, lay the mount aside. After you have finished mounting prints, wash off the glass and cleanse the brush.

Please set the mounts up separately to dry.

Let me suggest at this point, before I forget it, a handy appliance for mounting, or, in other words, rolling down your prints after they have been pasted. It consists of a round turned stick, over which a piece of rubber tubing has been drawn to cover the surface and to fit tightly. Six inches would be a convenient length for the stick and tubing. Put a three-quarter inch screw in the center of each end of the stick. Bend a piece of stout wire in a half circle, and then twist the two ends so that the screws will go into the rings thus made as far as their heads. Passing the screw up to the heads, through these two ends, and turning them into the ends of the stick, you will have a handy implement for rolling down the prints after they are laid on the mount.

Should the occasion arise when you desire to mount a picture on very thin card-board or on paper, the following special material should be used if you would have the prints, when dry, lay flat and be free from puckers:

Take of Nelson's No. 1 gelatine four ounces; water, sixteen ounces. Allow the gelatine to soak in the water for ten minutes, then set the bottle containing it in hot water to make the gelatine dissolve, after which add one ounce of glycerine, and then five ounces of alcohol. With the paste thus made there will be no trouble about mounting prints according to the previous directions in this chapter. This paste re-

FIG. 26.

quires warming (by setting the bottle in hot water) before use. Whether the mounted prints shall be framed or put in a portfolio, is left to the taste of the amateur.

As neat an arrangement as I have ever seen for holding pictures, consists of a pair of covers made with expanding backs, so that from six to twenty-four pictures may be inserted in one cover. Figure 26 represents the cover, with perforations in the back, through which the spreading clasps of the paper fastener bind the whole together. The pictures are mounted in the usual way, and strips of linen or strong paper of the proper width are pasted on one edge, through holes in which, as just intimated, paper fasteners are inserted. These can easily be put in or taken out. The whole arrangement is simple and will be comprehended at a glance. For binding together views, a series or set of landscapes, or photographs of any kind, they are very serviceable.

CHAPTER X.

In summer keep your solutions cool; also use cold water in washing the gelatine plates.

In winter keep your solutions from freezing.

Should crystallization appear on a negative after it is dry, it shows a failure to thoroughly wash the negative before drying.

Do not use the fixing pan for any other purpose than to hold the hypo. solution. Label the pan *Hypo.*, so that there will be no mistake.

Always wash your hands after using the hyposulphite of soda solution, and before handling another plate.

After removal from the fixing solution, the negative must have the hyposulphite of soda thoroughly washed out of the film. *This is important.*

All trays and measures should be washed out after developing each plate.

Should you pour too much iron solution into the oxalate solution it will cause a yellow precipitate to form. Always add the iron to the oxalate, and do not reverse the order, or the same trouble will ensue.

Never fail to pour clear water over the plate before developing. If you follow this direction, disagreeable markings, resulting from a stoppage in the flow of the developer, will be avoided, and at the same time air bubbles, which cause transparent spots in the negative, will be prevented.

A plate varnished before it is thoroughly dry has a milky appearance.

Keep sensitized plates in a cool, dry place; dampness causes them to mildew.

Clear negatives cannot be produced with an alkaline sample of oxalate of potash.

Bromide in the developer restrains its action, but too much destroys detail in the shadows.

If negatives show too much contrast between the light and the dark portions, weaken the developer by the addition of water.

By taking an extra ground glass when going far away from a base of supplies, should the one in use get broken, the second one will be a welcome substitute.

Under-exposure gives clear shadows, but the picture produced from the negative is wanting in detail, and has a hard appearance.

Dust off the surface of gelatine plates with a soft camel's hair brush. The so-called pin holes in the negative are caused by dust. In this connection it will be well to add, keep the camera, lens and holder well dusted out, for no evil effect will result from it. Quite the reverse.

CHAPTER XI.

ALTHOUGH the art beautiful has some conspicuous and skillful devotees in an amateur way among the ladies, the time and appliances have not been ripe until now for popularizing this recreation among them. To have mastered a science or art, when the difficulties surrounding it have not been conquered by genius, is praiseworthy, and therefore much credit is due to the pioneer picture makers of the fair sex. The same results that they achieved, and better, can now be obtained by perfected appliances which I am about to describe.

If amateur photography is pleasant with the environment shown in the illustration on the following page, can the gentler sex resist an accomplishment which henceforth may combine the maximum of grace and fascination? Here, as well as abroad, amateur photography is destined to be taken up by ladies of refinement and quick artistic perception. The "tyrant man" will not be needed to carry about a pocket outfit, consisting of a 4 x 5 camera, accompanying dry plate holder, and an extension tripod, weighing complete but three and three-quarter pounds.

Figure No. 27 depicts a pocket camera when folded up. Such cameras are made in two sizes, viz., 4 x 5 and 5 x 8 inches. This recently patented pocket camera is provided with brass pieces hinged to the frame of the camera, and movable, so that they may be either folded down upon the side of the camera, or swung out to button on to the camera front, when it is drawn out and the bellows extended. No little pains and ingenuity were expended to combine utility with compactness. The resulting apparatus looks so simple

that one is tempted to exclaim, "Any one could have con-
trived that." Many have tried to make pocket cameras,
but have succeeded only in name, not in reality.
This 4 x 5 pocket camera, when folded up compactly, is but one and three-quarter inches thick,
which is not more space than an ordinary book oc-
cupies. No case is needed to stow it in and take it
about. The aforesaid being of the sterner sex will undoubt-

FIG. 27.

edly put such a camera away in one pocket, and the plate
holders in another. It would be quite *recherché* for the ladies
to use for this purpose a hand satchel or velvet bag. The
latter especially might be made very handsome, and at the
same time so as to be used for a focusing cloth.

Another new pocket camera, for which application for a patent
has been made, is provided with *lazy tong levers*, which permit
the front to be drawn out for focusing, to be swung up or
down ; there is also considerable freedom of motion to one
side or the other. Either style of camera is made of mahogany,
finished in the finest style. The bellows are of a purplish
hue, wonderfully harmonizing with the mahogany and
polished brass-work of the camera. The flange on the front
board has a thread cut inside in such a manner as to permit
the lens, when not in use, to be screwed on inside, and thus to
be neatly stowed away in the camera. American lenses are
the best to use in connection with pocket cameras.

Accompanying the pocket cameras are single dry plate
holders, which well deserve mention. Figure 28 illustrates one

of them. Upon the stopper to the slide a catch is
set which hooks into an eye on the frame of the
holder. At the pleasure of the initiated amateur,
the catch may be unset, and the slide drawn out.

FIG. 28.

The movable back of this incomparable plate holder has rabbeted edges, which slide under grooves in the edge of the frame,
and a spring at the top of the plate holder holds the back in
place.

Another spring on the under surface of the back keeps the
plate in focus, and also serves to throw out the back after it
has, by upward pressure of the hands on its outer surface,

been moved far enough to allow the rabbeted edge to slide out from under the edge of the holder. This holder will serve alike for use in the studio and for outdoor work.

FIG. 29.

The tripod, devised especially for use with pocket outfits, is not intended to be put in any pocket, unless it be those possessed by people of the stature of the Chinese giant; but, when its extension legs are drawn up, it is quite compact, and in height but two feet nine inches.

Glance at figure 29. The button on each leg of the tripod may be turned at pleasure, thus shortening or lengthening them, and giving with celerity any incline needed for the camera by a very easy method. Such a tripod does not unjoint. Where's the necessity of it? In a flash it can be gotten ready for use, and there is no part to be detached and lost.

Because these pocket cameras and holders are so compact, men in business or for pleasure excursions will make use of them. There need be no quarrel as to who shall possess such cameras.

Ladies and gentlemen alike or together might share in their use and the pleasure they may afford. Some of the amateur photographic societies now forming will do a graceful act by inviting ladies to their membership. This latter will seem like a dissertation, and without question it is.

Rather to you, reader, should be assigned the duty of arousing enthusiasm for the art, and winning to it votaries fair and gentle.

CHAPTER XII.

PLATES sometimes commence to pucker at the edge. This is called "*frilling.*" Should it show itself at any stage of the manipulation, immediately remove the recalcitrant plate and flow over its surface a saturated solution of alum, wash the plate, and proceed from the point where you left off. A strong solution of hyposulphite of soda often causes frilling; so do warm solutions, and treating the negative with a weak solution of acids.

Over-exposed plates, if not properly controlled in the developing, have a foggy appearance, and they make weak prints.

If the edge of the plates, which were protected by the grooves in the holder, remain clear, then fogging comes from lack of care in developing.

When a plate is under-exposed its shadows are clear, but weak.

Negatives which require a long time to fix show one of two things: either the hyposulphite of soda solution is too strong or too weak. About one ounce of the soda to six ounces of water is a safe rule to go by in making this solution.

Negatives from which a number of prints are required must be varnished, or otherwise they will turn red from a combination of the free silver in the sensitized paper with the gelatine film of the negative. Exposed plates may be kept some weeks before developing, but the better plan is to do this as soon as possible after taking the view.

Should a plate by accident be exposed to light, it may possibly be recovered for service in the following manner: In two ounces of water dissolve twenty grains bichromate of potash. Into this solution lay the light-struck plate for five minutes—*of course, this is done in the dark room*. At the expiration of the time, it is taken out of the solution and washed in several changes of fresh water, and set up to dry by ruby light. When dry the plate is ready to be placed in a plate holder and exposed. If not to be used, pack the plate away where concealed from light.

When a plate is exposed in the camera, and you are certain that the result is not good, as, for instance, in taking a group of which one or more of the figures moved, put the plate through the mild course of treatment just described, and it may be rejuvenated for use a second time, with a more successful result.

Mistakes in timing an exposure are many. The professional photographer may err. If the calculation cannot be made with certainty, have the error on the side of over- rather than under-exposure, as the former can be controlled in the development.

Too much density in a negative can be reduced by flowing over the film, after it has been washed with water, the following solution: *Water, six ounces; chloride of iron, one drachm*. If the reduction is to be only a slight one, make the proportion of water greater. After a brief period wash the negative and place it in the fixing solution once more, then wash it well to remove the hypo., and set the negative up to dry. Should only small portions of the negative require reducing, wash the plate, after which, with care, apply the reducer to the parts requiring it with a soft brush, and then wash the plate and put it in the fixing solution.

Density in a negative may be increased in this way: After the detail is brought out with the oxalate developer you are using, pour it off and flow over the plate the old oxalate developer mentioned on page 34, containing three grains to the ounce of bromide of potassium. If after this treatment you still lack the density you require, fix the plate in a solution made up as follows: Dissolve one ounce of protosulphate of iron in three ounces of water. In another bottle dissolve one ounce of hyposulphite of soda in three ounces of water. Mix the two solutions in a tray, permit them to stand a while, and then immerse the negative in the mingled solutions. After fixing, wash and dry the negative.

Note books afford a means of recording everything essential relating to the exposure of a plate in the camera. Do not fail to make use of them, as admonished in a previous chapter. Compare the results, and try to avoid a repetition of the least desirable ones. Number your negatives to correspond with the book.

How to Make Transparencies.—In the dark room, illuminated by ruby light, place a negative, film side up, in the printing frame; on the surface of the negative lay a gelatine plate of the slow kind, film side down. (For this purpose special plates are prepared and sold.) Put the back in the printing frame, fasten the springs, and cover the frame with the focusing cloth, taking it into a room where a gas or kerosene light is burning. Hold the frame with the negative toward the light, and distant about twelve inches from it. Take off the focusing cloth, give from ten to twenty seconds' exposure, according to the density of the negative; re-cover the printing frame, and go back to the dark room. Use the following developer for the gelatine plate:

No. 1.

Neutral oxalate of potash, - - 4 *ounces.*
Water, - - - - - 20 "
Bromide of potassium, - - 40 *grains.*
*A saturated solution of oxalic or citric acid
(enough to turn blue litmus paper red).*

No. 2.

Sulphate of iron, - - - 300 *grains.*
Water, - - - - - 3 *ounces.*

Take of solution No. 1, seven ounces; and of No. 2 solu-

tion one ounce.   Mix them, and develop until the detail in the
highly lighted portion shows quite plainly.   The result should
be a fine positive picture or transparency, which is fixed,
washed, and dried, and then is ready to be put in a nickel-
plated frame with a ground glass at the back, and hung where
the light shines through it—probably to adorn a window.

Magic Lantern Slides.—To make these slides, proceed in a similar manner to that just described for making transparencies, observing care, however, not to get the positive too
dense, or, in other words, so opaque that light shining through
it will not throw out all the details in the picture.   In short,
the positive should be weak, but its details perfect, in order to
make a fine lantern slide.

Fogging.—Fogging, as defined by Lake Price, "is an
opaque film covering a negative, which obliterates the forms,
preventing them from being clearly distinguished in whatever
direction they may be viewed."   Thomas Sutton writes thus
concerning it : " When a precipitate is thrown over the entire
plate by the action of the developer, so as to obscure in the
deepest shadows the transparency of the glass when looked
through, it is fog."   The causes of fog are many.   It may
result from white light falling on the sensitive plate.

Another cause is defective development.

Another, hyposulphite of soda getting in the developer.

Or chemicals put on the plate from the hands, which were
not washed.

Or trying to force the development of an under-exposed
plate.

Not properly modifying the developer for an over-exposed
plate.

Using an alkaline sample of oxalate of potash.

Or exposing plates in an old holder having free silver
about it.

When troubled with fog, examine the gelatine plate, and if
the edges which were protected by the rabbeted edge of the
holder are clear, the fault is chargeable to the development, as

the plate was evidently over-exposed and the developer not modified to meet the case. If the fog is all over the plate, it may have come from white lights, from an alkaline oxalate, from under-exposure and forcing the development.

WEIGHTS AND MEASURES.

APOTHECARIES' WEIGHT.

SOLID MEASURE.

20 Grains   = 1 Scruple = ℈
3 Scruples = 1 Drachm = ℨ
8 Drachms = 1 Ounce = ℥
12 Ounces = 1 Pound = ℔

FLUID.

60 Minims = 1 Fluid Drachm ℨ
8 Drachms = 1 Ounce   ℥
20 Ounces = 1 Pint.
8 Pints   = 1 Gallon.

The above weights are those usually adopted in formulas, and are what are used in the foregoing chapters. As the amateur advances in the picture making art, he will, without doubt, read up in photographic literature, a course which cannot be too highly commended.

He will also be inclined to experiment a little. It is an undisputed fact that to the amateur photography owes fully as much for progress and inventive skill as to the professional photographer.

Photography in England is indebted, during many years past, for improvements and discoveries almost wholly to the amateur's researches and experiments. It is safe to assert that the amateur in this country will rival his brother across the water in the display of ingenuity.

In trying different formulas, many of which are written by

the French standard of weights and measures, the following tables will save a considerable amount of figuring, bother, and failure.

French Fluid Measures. — The cubic centimeter, usually represented by "c. c.," is the unit of the French measurement for liquids. It contains nearly seventeen minims of water; in reality it contains 16.896 minims. The weight of this quantity of water is one gramme. Hence it will be seen that the cubic centimeter and the gramme bear to each other the same relation as our drachms for solids and the drachms for fluids, or as the minim and the grain. The following table will prove to be sufficiently accurate for phototographic purposes:

1 cubic centimeter	=	17 minims (as near as possible).								
2 cubic centimeters	=	34	"							
3 "	=	51	"							
4 "	=	68	"	or 1 drachm	8 minims.					
5 "	=	85	"	" 1 "	25	"				
6 "	=	102	"	" 1 "	42	"				
7 "	=	119	"	" 1 "	59	"				
8 "	=	136	"	" 2 drachms	16	"				
9 "	=	153	"	" 2 "	33	"				
10 "	=	170	"	" 2 "	50	"				
20 "	=	340	"	" 5 "	40	"				
30 "	=	510	"	" 1 ounce	0 drachm	30 minims.				
40 "	=	680	"	" 1 "	3 drachms	20	"			
50 "	=	850	"	" 1 "	6 "	10	"			
60 "	=	1020	"	" 2 ounces	1 "	0	"			
70 "	=	1190	"	" 2 "	3 "	50	"			
80 "	=	1360	"	" 2 "	6 "	40	"			
90 "	=	1530	"	" 3 "	1 "	30	"			
100 "	=	1700	"	" 3 "	4 "	20	"			

The Conversion of French into English Weight. —Although a gramme is equal to 15.4346 grains, the decimal is one which can never be used by photographers; hence, in the following table it is assumed to be 15⅔ grains, which is the nearest approach that can be made to *practical* accuracy:

1	gramme	=	$15\frac{2}{5}$	grains.				
2	grammes	=	$30\frac{4}{5}$	"				
3	"	=	$46\frac{1}{5}$	"				
4	"	=	$61\frac{3}{5}$	"	or	1 drachm	$1\frac{3}{5}$	grain.
5	"	=	77	"	"	1 "	17	grains.
6	"	=	$92\frac{2}{5}$	"	"	1 "	$32\frac{2}{5}$	"
7	"	=	$107\frac{4}{5}$	"	"	1 "	$47\frac{4}{5}$	"
8	"	=	$123\frac{1}{5}$	"	"	2 drachms	$3\frac{1}{5}$	"
9	"	=	$138\frac{3}{5}$	"	"	2 "	$18\frac{3}{5}$	"
10	"	=	154	"	"	2 "	34	"
11	"	=	$169\frac{2}{5}$	"	"	2 "	$49\frac{2}{5}$	"
12	"	=	$184\frac{4}{5}$	"	"	3 "	$4\frac{4}{5}$	"
13	"	=	$200\frac{1}{5}$	"	"	3 "	$20\frac{1}{5}$	"
14	"	=	$215\frac{3}{5}$	"	"	3 "	$35\frac{3}{5}$	"
15	"	=	231	"	"	3 "	51	"
16	"	=	$246\frac{2}{5}$	"	"	4 "	$6\frac{2}{5}$	"
17	"	=	$261\frac{4}{5}$	"	"	4 "	$21\frac{4}{5}$	"
18	"	=	$277\frac{1}{5}$	"	"	4 "	$37\frac{1}{5}$	"
19	"	=	$292\frac{3}{5}$	"	"	4 "	$52\frac{3}{5}$	"
20	"	=	308	"	"	5 "	8	"
30	"	=	462	"	"	7 "	42	"
40	"	=	616	"	"	10 "	16	"
50	"	=	770	"	"	12 "	50	"
60	"	=	924	"	"	15 "	24	"
70	"	=	1078	"	"	17 "	58	"
80	"	=	1232	"	"	20 "	32	"
90	"	=	1386	"	"	23 "	6	"
100	"	=	1540	"	"	25 "	40	"

Measuring with a Glass Graduate.—On the graduated glass you will find lines and figures as shown by the diagram on next page. The figures 1, 2, 3 and 4 on the left hand of the center line represent ounces, and so also does the mark ℥ designate the same. The short lines between the ounce lines, 1, 2, 3, 4, represent half ounces. On the lower right hand side of the center line you will find the figures 2, 4, 6, 8. These represent drachms; and the mark or character ʒ is used to denote drachms. Example: To measure two ounces and six drachms, fill the graduate to the line with figure 2 at left hand side, pour this out into the vessel designed for the solution, then fill the graduate to the line with figure 6 on the right hand side; this is six drachms. Add this to the two ounces just measured, which gives you two ounces and six drachms.

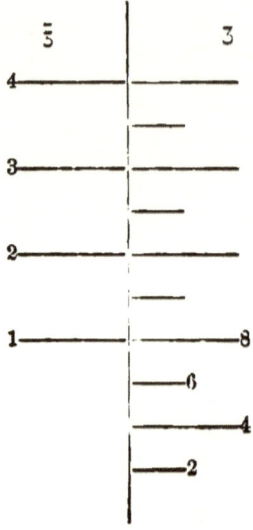

CHAPTER XIII.

CONSIDERABLE is heard about instantaneous photography at the present time. It is a subject that interests every one. When made practicable the photographer eagerly seized hold of the lightning process, applied it in taking the pictures of babies and restless children, and in many other ways.

It is enough to lure any one into amateur photography, the very thought of picturing animated objects distinctly, with all the appearance of motion instantly arrested.

The amateur may infer that the appliances for securing instantaneous pictures are very complicated. Not at all! It is necessary to use gelatine plates of great sensitiveness. These are regularly kept on hand by dealers in photographic goods. The second requisite is that the lens used on the camera should be provided with a drop, as shown in figure 8, and described on page 18; or else that instantaneous shutters be fitted on to the lens or camera. The day chosen for taking the picture should be a bright one, and the time between ten A.M. and two P.M. is much to be preferred. See that the object to be photographed is brightly illuminated on the side toward the camera.

Suppose a passing steamboat first calls into use the instantaneous drop on a lens you possess. Your ambition is suddenly awakened when the boat looms up in the distance, and you plant the tripod and point the camera toward where it will soon pass. Judge how far it will be away from you as it glides by, and obtain an approximate focus for this distance.

If possible, focus upon an object as remote as the steamboat will be in passing the point where the picture is to be taken. Secure the focus by this method, or by using your own judgment. If the drop is not already in the lens put it in, and hold it up by a turn of the button underneath the lens. Substitute a holder for the ground glass.

As the steamboat is now near at hand, draw out the dark slide separating the sensitive plate from the camera, and lay it on top of the latter. Stand behind the camera, grasping the cord attached to the button holding up the instantaneous drop.

Keep cool as an old hunter, glance your eyes over the top of the camera, and when the boat arrives at a point directly in the line that the lens points to, pull the cord. As the opening in the drop passes through the lens the light flashes through the aperture to the gelatine plate, and the image is impressed there. Is there any other demonstration needed of the rapidity with which light travels? The amateur may have been nervous, and have pulled the cord too soon. Instead of the whole steamboat, he finds but the forward half of it when the picture is brought out; or, on the other hand, only the stern and the wake of the boat may be caught.

Sport, like shooting at birds in their flight, cannot be more exciting and exhilarating. If the amateur "shoots" at a steamboat with his camera and hits a barge, he will succeed better upon the next trial. The fall of the instantaneous drop by the law of gravitation will do for the first attempt. After a time the amateur will scheme and contrive, by the use of an elastic band over the top of the drop or by some other device, to shorten the exposure. The ambition to reduce the time from one-tenth to one-thousandth part of a second and less is similar to that of turfmen in striving to have their racers excel all previous records of time.

Shooting yachts that are dashing along through the waves under full sail is a favorite accomplishment of the full-fledged amateur. The beauty and life of the yacht may be portayed perfectly.

The only cautions I have to give are, do not attempt too much at first in instantaneous work; and the other piece of advice relates to the development of gelatine plates exposed but for a fractional part of a second. More care is needed than for the ordinary plates. My plan is to mix a fresh developer for each plate, consisting of two ounces of oxalate of potash solution and a quarter of an ounce of the iron solution. Should this prove too weak, more iron solution may be added, but do not put in too much. When the details are brought out, pour off the developer, and flow over the plate some of the old oxalate developer as described on page 34. This will give density without danger of fogging the plate. Wash and fix, then wash and dry. After the negative is dry, if on examination it requires to be strengthened, proceed as follows: Lay the plate, film side up, in a tray containing clear water, while you mix the intensifying solution. In thirty-two ounces of water (one quart) dissolve one ounce of chloride of ammonia and one ounce chloride of mercury. Pour off the water from the plate and cover it with some of the above mercury solution diluted one-half with water (that is, an equal part of the solution and water). Leave this on the plate until it has uniformly whitened, which will take but a few seconds, then pour it off and wash the plate well. Also rinse out the tray, into which replace the plate, film side up.

Take four ounces of water, and to it add one drachm of liquid ammonia. Pour this on the plate so it flows quickly and evenly over it. The negative will turn dark brown. As soon as it has done so, remove it from the tray, wash, and set it up to dry.

Throw away the ammonia solution, and wash out the tray.

Developing solutions for instantaneous exposures, to be used when a more energetic developer than the ferrous oxalate is necessary:

P.—Citric acid, - - - -	60 grains.	
Water, - - - - - -	7 ounces.	
Dissolve, and add		
Pyrogallic acid, - - -	1 ounce.	
Water sufficient to make measure	10 ounces.	
A.—Liquor ammonia, - - - -	2 "	
Water, - - - - -	8 "	
B.—Bromide of ammonium or potassium,	1 ounce.	
Water, to make - - - -	10 ounces.	

DEVELOPMENT.—Add one ounce solution P. to thirteen ounces water; one ounce solution A. and one ounce solution B. to twelve ounces water. Mix equal parts of each for developing. Two ounces of each will be ample for a 5 x 8 or 6½ x 8½ plate, to be mixed just before laying plate in the developing dish. Flow the developer by a gentle motion over the plate. The image soon appears and, if correctly exposed, will attain full density in sixty to ninety seconds. Allow development to proceed till the detail in the deepest shadows is well brought out.

Allusion was made in the introductory chapter to taking pictures of horses while they were speeding around the race track. The method by which this was accomplished has been so often described that repetition is unnecessary. Some achievements last summer of the well-known veteran photographic journalist, Mr. J. Traill Taylor, deserve mention. From the deck of a steamer plying out to a pleasure retreat on Long Island Sound, he "shot" at and secured the pictures of yachts skimming along in an opposite course. Again, on Boston Bay, in a little steamer that tossed about like a cockleshell, the temptation to point his lens at some passing boats could not be resisted, so he did not try to withstand the allurement. It was of no use to fasten the camera on to the tripod; better sea legs were required, and these were supplied by the photographic *litterateur*. Placing the camera under one arm, at the right moment he touched the trigger, releasing the instantaneous drop, light flashed through the lens and fixed upon the sensitive plate the impression of an animated marine view. Pity the man who could not appreciate such sport. In his journalistic capacity, Mr. Taylor may be called upon to record many skillful instantaneous shots made by men who, after reading this, will strive to outdo him with feats more wonderful than his.

CHAPTER XIV

How to Make and Mount Them.—The camera used to make stereoscopic pictures should take a 5 x 8-inch plate in the holder, have an upright division through the center, and upon the front board a pair of matched view lenses screwed into the flanges. Such are the requisites for this special service. Make sure that the central partition, called a stereo. division, is fastened in place.

Some discernment is needed in selecting the subject for a stereoscopic view. If the camera points to a distant hillside, and there is no near object included in the range, the view will appear flat when seen through the stereoscope, and will not seem to stand out from the mount. There should be included in the image reflected on the ground glass a near as well as the more remote view. Some shrubbery, the stump of a tree, or any distant and still object will answer. Stereo. pictures made upon this principle have the most seeming actuality about them. If the two pictures seen upon the ground glass are exactly alike, it is a proof that the lenses in use are well matched. After focusing, put the plate holder up in place of the ground glass.

As it is essential to success that the exposure of the two lenses should be made at the same time, place the focusing cloth on top of the camera, falling over to cover the lenses, and keep the cloth tightly drawn over them. Pull out the dark slide and, as usual, lay it on top of the camera. Now, all is in readiness. Raise the focusing cloth quickly. Do this so that light will enter the apertures in the lenses simultaneously. After a proper length of exposure, drop the focusing cloth

over the lenses and replace the dark slide.   Follow directions
in Chapter IV. for the development of the plate, but use care
not to get one side of it more intense than the other; in short,
the negative should be treated the same as any other, until it
is ready to be printed from.   Take a piece of ground glass, a
trifle larger than the stereo. negative, and upon it draw with a

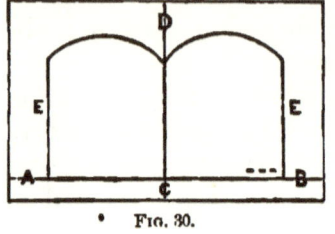

lead pencil the diagram shown in
figure 30.

The distance between each of
the lines E and the perpendicular
D C should be 3½ inches, and
from the base line to the crown
of both arches, 3¾ inches.

* Fig. 30.

These proportions make the
very desirable size of stereo pictures, commonly called the
"*artistic.*"

Lay the negative, film side up, upon the marked ground
glass so that the right-hand half will come over the right-hand
form penciled thereon, and *vice versa*.   Take in the best portion of the subject.   With care move the negative so that the
line A B will pass through similar objects in both halves; also
adjust the negative to have the perpendicular C D pass through
defined lines or objects in the right half.   With a sharp-
pointed instrument scratch on the negative, using a straight-
edged ruler, the line A B, also the line E.   Shift the negative
so that the perpendicular C D will intersect points or objects
corresponding to those in the other half.   At the same time
the scratched base line must coincide with, or be directly
above, the line A B on the ground glass.   Now, scratch the
left-hand line E, and the negative will be ready for printing.

All of the prints made will show a black base line, and the
two outside ones, E E.   Turn the prints face downward, and
upon the back of the right-hand half mark with a pencil the
letter L, and on the left-hand picture the letter R.   Now,
reverse the prints to have the face upward.   It is to be hoped
that you have available a glass form 3¼ inches wide by 3¾
inches high, with an arch top.   Set down this form upon each
print alternately, so that the lower edge will be on the line A

B, and one side on one of the lines *E*. With a sharp knife or a *Robinson trimmer* cut closely around the form. The Robinson trimmer is suggested because it is so desirable that it has the commendation of photographers everywhere. Always cut the prints on a light of glass.

In mounting the prints on the card, put the one marked *L* on the left-hand side, and the one marked *R* on the right side, and have the two edges meet in the center of the card; also have an equal margin above and below the pictures. If you can avail yourself of a printing press or hand stamp with movable type, and choose to do so, you can print on fine tissue paper the name of the picture or locality of the view. In printing from the negative, this piece of tissue paper is laid on the face of the negative in one corner, so that the lettering will copy on to the print in the place shown by dotted lines on figure 30. Thin tissue or onion-skin paper will not prevent the printing of any part of the negative—the effect is to make the operation a slower one.

The instruction contained in this chapter will be pronounced quite elementary by men of experience. The reasons why have not been given, but enough is stated to enable the amateur to secure good results.

Indeed, the same is true of all that precedes, and I do not imagine that any one will think that he has mastered all there is in photography after fortifying by experience the teachings of this book.

The purpose is to enable the amateur to meet with success, and to furnish a stepping stone by which books more technical and profound will be made intelligible and interesting to the non-professional photographer. Very few, I think, will be satisfied with the rudiments of *this truly fascinating art*.

CHAPTER XV.

THE microscopist needs a convenient method to enable him to easily and correctly reproduce the result of his observations. Granted that this is now practicable, it follows that greater interest in microscopy itself must be awakened, and pathological, entomological and many branches of study and research be wonderfully aided by the addition of a camera as a reporter and recorder, so to speak. As I am in microscopy but a novice, though with growing interest, I will quote what is said on this subject in the July number of the *Photographic Times and American Photographer*.

Photographing with the microscope has hitherto been accomplished by the aid of elaborate and costly apparatus, and been applied chiefly to making illustrations for scientific magazines. The process used, that of wet collodion in connection with sunlight, involved the procurement of an expensive heliostat to produce a steady illumination, for with any less powerful light the exposure would necessarily be so prolonged that the coating of the plate would dry and become useless. Now all this is changed, for with the modern improvements in photography which are the result of the introduction of gelatine dry plates, the photographing of microscopic objects becomes as easy of accomplishment as the photographing of the beautiful and visible in nature is with the popular amateur outfits. I therefore propose briefly, yet fully, to describe how it can be done by means of an inexpensive outfit. The scientist and microscopist, instead of spending hours in making imperfect drawings, aided by the camera lucida, may in a few minutes, with the assistance of photography, produce a more perfect representation of a minute object than it is possible for the hand of man to do, working conjointly with the eye. Not only can an enlarged image of a microscopic object be formed for illustration, but professors in colleges will find it a ready means to produce negatives of a suitable size from which may be made transparencies or magic lantern slides for exhibition to classes or the public.

The necessary requisites for those in possession of a microscope are a suitable artificial light, a half-plate camera made for this purpose, gelatine dry plates, and chemicals for development.

The Scovill Manufacturing Company have, with their usual promptness to meet any new and real want in the art-science of photography, constructed a suitable camera of a size to use what are known as the half and quarter plates. The writer has devised and patented a lantern for dry plate use, which by the addition of a condenser furnishes a light for use with the microscope, and its convenience is such that when arranged

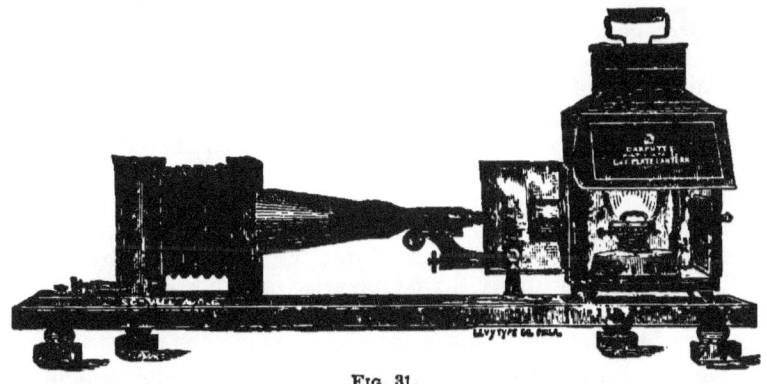

FIG. 31.

with the microscope and camera (as shown in figure 31) it furnishes a clear, strong light for photographing, and then a red or non-actinic light for developing the exposed plates, without any change but a half reversal of the lantern. If made use of in the daytime, a room from which all white light is excluded should be selected; but if used at night, as in most cases it would be, the operations may be all performed in the midst of a family group for their interest and amusement, and to impart to them knowledge of the minute life or organisms of the world which the microscope alone can reveal.

Having provided yourself with a photomicroscopic equipment, consisting of a multum in parvo lantern and condenser, a Scovill half-plate camera, some Keystone B plates, $4\frac{1}{4}$ x $5\frac{1}{2}$ size, to make negatives, also some A plates, $3\frac{1}{4}$ x $4\frac{1}{4}$ size, for transparencies, and the necessary chemicals, proceed to set up the apparatus. First, procure a board one inch thick, about four feet in length and a trifle wider than the camera. Screw battens on the under side in order to keep the upper surface flat and free from warping, tack on the sides a thin strip of wood, allowing it to project half an inch above the surface, so that camera, microscope and lantern can all be kept in line. To be successful, it will be necessary in arranging the apparatus for the first time to do so with care, so that it can at any future time be put in position without a waste of time. Place the baseboard on any flat surface—a table or bench—make four wooden wedges, place them under the sides near the end, and with a spirit level proceed to level the surface both in its width and length. Now, on the left hand end of the board place the camera; in the middle of the board place the microscope, with the tube set horizontally; see if the eyepiece centers with the center of the camera. If it does not and is lower, place a thin board under the microscope or raise it till its center corresponds to the center of the camera, and then proceed to test the tube of the microscope by placing the level on it in the direction of its length; if not level it must be made so by any suitable means that can be applied to it. If the microscope is found to center with the camera as it rests on the baseboard, a ready means of placing it in position at any future time is to mark exactly where it stands and thus save future calculations. Adjust the lantern so that the diaphragm of the condenser centers with and is in line with the objective of the microscope, then finally, by connecting the tube of the microscope with the cone of the camera, at the end of which is a sleeve of rubber cloth, the apparatus is ready for use.

I have somewhat minutely described the first arrangement of the various parts, because neglect of a proper adjustment at the beginning might result in failure. When arranged as described, and the position of each marked for future guidance, these parts are easily and quickly put together at any future time, and the baseboard can be placed on any convenient support. I use and recommend as guards against jarring, four hard rubber balls placed in the sunken center of four small blocks of wood, as shown in figure 31.

Now, all being ready, light the lamp, after filling the reservoir not more than two-thirds full with good head light oil; trim the wick square on the top, let it burn a few minutes, then adjust the wick for a bright but not too high flame. Turn the lamp by the button underneath so that the reflector throws the light through the door without the porcelain screen at the left side of the lantern; then unscrew the burner a little and turn it so that a perspective view of the flame is presented to the eye when on a line with the camera and microscope; adjust the reflector so that the center of reflection coincides with the center of the white part of the flame (this can be done by temporarily removing the sliding back of lantern); then place in position the condenser by slipping the frame under the upper metal strip in the left hand opening and bending the lower metal strip against it. Put the object to be photographed on the stage of the microscope; first see that a sharp disc of light is formed on the ground glass of the camera; it may require, and most likely will, a forward or lateral adjustment of the lantern with its condenser to get the best light effect, and when this is obtained mark on the baseboard for future guidance. Proceed to arrange the size of the picture by looking at the image on the ground glass and focus with the coarse adjustment, first removing the eyepiece.

After having got the image of suitable size, I advise the following mode of final focusing: Take a piece of clear flat glass of the same size as the gelatine plate, place this in the holder with the back and slide taken out, and with a magnifier adjusted to the surface of the glass, proceed to focus with this fine adjustment; then, by ruby light, replace the plain glass by a sensitive gelatine plate—of course replacing the slide and back—place it on the camera, and with a piece of card temporarily cut off the light: withdraw the slide and allow the light to act for 45, 90 or 120 seconds, according to the object and amount of amplification. One or two trials is the only way of arriving at a correct judgment of the requisite exposure. With a one to three inch microscopic objective I have found the time to average as above quoted, and that the color of the object influences this greatly, one strong in color—such as most insect specimens—requiring from 60 to 90 seconds, using a one to two inch double system objective. The exposure being made, the development and finishing of the negative is conducted as described in the preceding chapters of this book.

Many thanks are due to my good friend Mr. Carbutt for his kindly suggestions, as they hastened the completion of an equipment which in my sincere belief answers a long felt want. and will aid materially in scientific investigation with the microscope, bring the results before the eyes and to the understanding of a far greater number than ever before, and indeed develop another and new form of social or home entertainment.

CONTENTS.

INTRODUCTORY CHAPTER.
PAGE

Amateur Photography, its scope and uses, - - - - 5

CHAPTER I.

Description of Apparatus, the cheapest and also the finest, - - 11

CHAPTER II.

Filling the Plate Holders in the Darkened Room, - - - - 20

CHAPTER III.

Taking the Picture, - - - - - - - - - 24

CHAPTER IV.

Development of Gelatine Plates, - - - - - - - 28

CHAPTER V.

Fixing Gelatine Plates; also treating on Over-exposure, and describing a Stock Developing Bottle, - - - - - - - 31

CHAPTER VI.

Varnishing the Negative, - - - - - - - - 36

CHAPTER VII.

Printing from the Negative, - - - - - - - 38

CONTENTS.

CHAPTER VIII

PAGE

Toning and Fixing Prints—Blue Prints, how to make them, - - 40

CHAPTER IX.

Trimming and Mounting Prints, - - - - - - - 43

CHAPTER X.

Items to be Borne in Mind, - - - - - - - 46

CHAPTER XI.

Photography for Ladies, - - - - - - - - 48

CHAPTER XII.

Useful Information, treating on varied topics, Fogging among them; describing how to make Transparencies and Magic Lantern Slides; also giving Tables of Weights and Measures, - - 51

CHAPTER XIII.

Instantaneous Photography, - - - - - - - 59

CHAPTER XIV.

Stereoscopic Pictures, how to make and mount them, - - - 63

CHAPTER XV.

Photography with the Microscope, - - - - 66

1

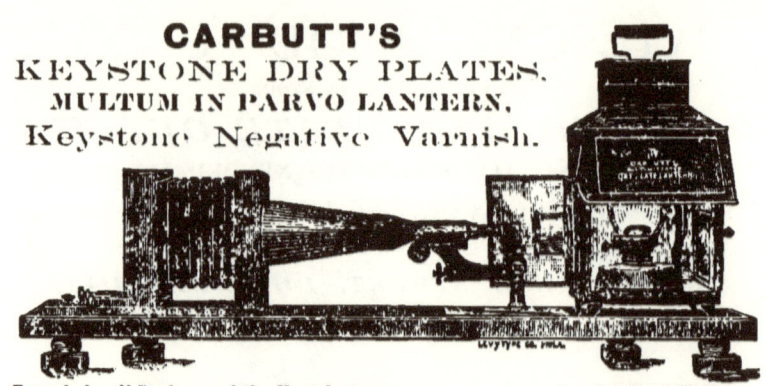
4

6

7

8

9

THE
SCOVILL
Portable
DRY PLATE OUTFITS
FOR AMATEURS.

Old Style Equipment.

New Style Equipment.

THE introduction of Dry Plates and the impetus given by them to the cause of Amateur Photography, created a demand for light and compact apparatus that could be easily carried about. That demand we anticipated and first met by the introduction of apparatus especially designed for the use of amateurs.

When we announced an Outfit comprising a Camera, Holder, Tripod, Carrying Case, and a good Lens, for $10, a new era in Amateur Photography began, and it is destined to be henceforth a popular and cultivating recreation.

The Cameras we make for amateurs are not mere toys—they have been used and approved by eminent photographers. Certainly no apparatus can compare with that made by our American Optical Co.'s Factory, in durability, accuracy and elegance of finish. It is in use in all parts of the globe, and has by merit won this wide-spread reputation. Be not deceived by what is copied after it. See that your apparatus bears the brand of our factory.

The NE PLUS ULTRA OUTFIT CAMERAS are warranted to produce pictures of the highest excellence ; they are accurate in every respect, and are made of white wood, stained in imitation of mahogany, or ebonized.

The 202 and '76 and 204 Cameras are made of selected Spanish mahogany, finished with a fine French polish. They have all the latest improvements ; swing back, folding bed, &c. For compactness, portability and style, there is nothing made equal to them.

Every article enumerated in this Catalogue has our guarantee.

10

SCOVILL'S
NE PLUS ULTRA APPARATUS OUTFITS,

All Articles of which are Warranted Accurate in Every Respect.

OUTFIT A, price $10 00, comprises

A VIEW CAMERA with rubber bellows and rigid platform, for making 4 x 5 inch pictures, with
1 Patent Double Dry Plate Holder, also
1 Folding Tripod.
1 "Waterbury" Achromatic Nickel Plated Lens.
1 Carrying Case.

OUTFIT B, price $12 00, comprises

A VIEW CAMERA, same style as A Camera for taking 5 x 8 inch pictures, with
1 Patent Double Dry Plate Holder, also
1 Folding Tripod.
1 "Waterbury" Achromatic Nickel Plated Lens.
1 Carrying Case.

OUTFIT C, price $18 50, comprises

A VIEW CAMERA for making 5 x 8 inch pictures.
This Camera is constructed so as to make either a *Cabinet Picture* on the full size of the plate (5 x 8 inches), or by substituting the extra front (supplied with the outfit) and using the pair of lenses of shorter focus, it is admirably adapted for taking *stereoscopic* negatives, also by the same arrangement two small pictures, 4 x 5 inches each, of dissimilar objects can be made on the one plate. Included in this outfit are also—
1 Patent Double Dry Plate Holder.
1 Large "Waterbury" Achromatic Nickel Plated Lens.
1 Pair "Waterbury" Achromatic Matched Stereoscopic Lenses.
1 Folding Tripod.
1 Carring Case.

OUTFIT D, price $13 50, comprises

1 VIEW CAMERA for making 6½ x 8½ inch pictures, with
1 Patent Double Dry Plate Holder, also
1 "Waterbury" Achromatic Nickel Plated Lens.
1 Folding Tripod.
1 Carrying Case.

EQUIPMENT A-A.

Consisting of APPARATUS OUTFIT A, with
1 Scovill Focusing Cloth.   1 W. I. A. Ruby Lantern.
1 dozen 4 x 5 Dry Plates.
          Complete for field service, Price, $12 25.

EQUIPMENT B-B.

Consisting of APPARATUS OUTFIT B, with
1 Scovill Focusing Cloth.   1 W. I. A. Ruby Lantern.
1 dozen 5 x 8 Dry Plates.
          Complete for field service, Price, $15 00.

EQUIPMENT C-C.

Consisting of APPARATUS OUTFIT C, with
1 Scovill Focusing Cloth.   1 W. I. A. Ruby Lantern.
1 dozen 5 x 8 Dry Plates.
          Complete for field service, Price, $21 50.

11

Scovill's Pure Chemicals

AND ACCESSORIES,
FOR MAKING NEGATIVES.

We offer for use with either N. P. U. Outfit "A," or A. O. Co. Outfits 202, the following goods packed securely in a wooden case :—

2 4 x 5 Japanned Pans,	1 lb. Alum,
1 4 oz. Graduate,	1 oz. Sulphuric Acid,
1 set 5 in. jap. Scales and Weights,	1 bottle Varnish,
1 oz. Bromide Ammonium,	1 doz. 4 x 5 Dry Plates,
1 lb. Neutral Oxalate Potash,	1 Scovill Note Book,
1 " Protosulphate Iron,	1 " Focusing Cloth,
1 " Hyposulphate Soda,	1 W. I. A. Ruby Lantern.

PRICE, COMPLETE, $6.50.

For use with N. P. U. Outfits "B" and "C," and A. O. Co. Outfit 203, we supply the same goods with the exception of the substitution of 5 x 8 Pans and Plates for the 4 x 5 size.

PRICE, COMPLETE, $7.50.

S. P. C. Ferro.-Prussiate Paper Outfit
For Printing and Mounting 4 x 5 Blue Print Pictures.

1 4 x 5 Printing Frame.	1 Glass Form (for trimming prints).
1 4½ x 5½ S. P. C. Vulcanite Pan.	1 Robinson's Straight Trimmer.
3 dozen 4 x 5 S. P. C. Ferro.-Prus-	¼ Pint Jar Parlor Paste.
siate Paper.	1 1 inch Paste Brush.
2 dozen sheets 6½ x 8½ Card-board.	

Price complete, $2 80. Securely packed in a Paper Box.

S. P. C.
Ferro-Prussiate Paper Outfit for Printing and Mounting 5 x 8 Blue Print Pictures.

This Outfit is like the one above, but with Printing Frame, Vulcanite Tray, Ferro.-Prussiate Paper, and Card-board adapted to 5 x 8 Pictures.

Price complete, $3 50. Securely packed in a Paper Box.

S. P. C.
Sensitized Albumen Paper Outfit for Printing, Toning, Fixing and Mounting 4 x 5 Pictures.

1 4 x 5 Printing Frame.	1 lb. Hyposulphate of Soda.
1 5 x 7 Porcelain Pan Deep.	2 dozen sheets 6½ x 8½ Card-board
1 5½ x 4½ S. P. C. Vulcanite Tray.	with Gilt Form.
2 dozen 5 x 8 S. P. C. Sensitized Al-	1 ¼ Pint Jar Parlor Paste.
bumen Paper.	1 1½ inch Bristle Brush.
1 bottle French Azotate,) for	1 Glass Form (for trimming prints).
1 " Chlor. Gold, 7½ gr. ∫ toning.	1 Robinson's Straight Trimmer.
1 2 Ounce Graduate.	

Price complete, $4 75. Securely packed in a Paper Box.

S. P. C.

Sensitized Albumen Paper Outfit for Printing, Toning, Fixing and Mounting 5 x 8 Pictures.

This Outfit is like the one above, but with Printing Frame, Vulcanite Tray, Sensitized Paper, and Card-board adapted for 5 x 8 Pictures.

Price complete, $6 00. Securely packed in a Paper Box.

EQUIPMENT A-A-A.

Complete in every Requisite for making the Highest Class Pictures.

Consisting of *Apparatus* Outfit A.................................$10 00
Also 1 *Chemical* Outfit 4 x 5..................................... 6 50
"   1 *Sensitized*   " 4 75

PRICE, $20.50.

EQUIPMENT B-B-B.

Complete in every Requisite for making the Highest Class Pictures.

Consisting of *Apparatus* Outfit B. $12 00
Also 1 *Chemical* Outfit 5 x 8...................................... 7 50
"   1 *Sensitized*   " 6 00

PRICE, $25.00.

EQUIPMENT C-C-C.

Complete in every Requisite for making the Highest Class Pictures.

Consisting of *Apparatus* Outfit C................................. $18 50
Also 1 *Chemical* Outfit 5 x 8...................................... 7 50
"   1 *Sensitized*   " 6 50

PRICE, $31.50.

Our **New PATENTED Double Dry Plate Holders** are the best made, and answer the demand in dry plate work for something that will exclude all light. Prices of EXTRA *Patent Double Dry Plate Holders* are as follows:

        4 x 5 Holders for two Plates....... ...each,$2 00
        5 x 8   "   "   ,   "   .... "   2 75
        6¼ x 8¼   "   "   "   .... "   4 25

Dry Plates, 4 x 5, per dozen, $0 95, 5 x 8, $1 80, 6¼ x 8¼, $2 40.

Extra Chemicals supplied at prevailing prices.

NEGATIVE BOXES.			SCOVILL OXALATE BOTTLE.		
4 x 5 .... Price, each,	$0	75	Pint............Price, each,	$0	60
5 x 8 .... "	"	1 00	Quart.......... "	"	0 75
6¼ x 8¼ .... "	"	1 10	Two Quarts.... "	"	1 00
			Gallon......... "	"	1 25

Scovill Focusing Glass............. ....each, $0 75
C. C. H.   "   "   .... "   4 00
Negative Washing Boxes................................... "   3 00

American Optical Company's Apparatus Outfits.

This apparatus is manufactured in New York City under our immediate personal supervision ; and, as we employ only highly skilled workmen, and use nothing but the choicest selected materials, we do not hesitate to assert that the products of our factory are unequaled in durability, excellence of workmanship, and style of finish. This fact is now freely conceded not only in this country but throughout Great Britain, Germany, Australia, and South America.

OUTFIT No. 202, price $27 00,

CONSISTS OF

A MAHOGANY POLISHED CAMERA for taking pictures 4 x 5 inches, with *Folding Bellows Body*, single swing, hinged bed, and brass guides. It has a shifting front for adjusting the sky and foreground, with
1 Patent Double Dry Plate Holder ; also,
1 Canvas Carrying Case.
1 Scovill Extension Tripod.

OUTFIT No. 203, price $41 00,

CONSISTS OF

A FOLDING MAHOGANY CAMERA, fully described in the American Optical

Company's Catalogue, and well known as the '76 Camera (see illustration.) It is adapted for taking 5 x 8 inch pictures, and also for stereoscopic views – together with
1 Patent Double Dry Plate Holder, also
1 Canvas Carrying Case.
1 Scovill Extension Tripod.

OUTFIT No. 204, price $50.00,

CONSISTS OF

A FOLDING MAHOGANY CAMERA of finest style and finish for taking 6¼ x 8¼ inch pictures, with
1 Double Dry Plate Holder, with
I Canvas Carrying Case.
1 Scovill Extension Tripod.

We recommend the purchase and use with the above outfits of a Lens or Lenses selected from the list on the next page.

Cameras for Photo-Micrography, Artist or Detective Cameras, and Pocket Cameras, made to order.

MORRISON'S
Wide-Angle View Lenses.

PATENTED MAY 21, 1872.

These Lenses are absolutely rectilinear; they embrace an angle of fully 100 degrees, and are the most rapid *wide-angle* lenses made. We recommend them for use with the foregoing outfits.

PRICE OF MORRISON'S WIDE-ANGLE LENSES.

								Price.
No. 1,	¼ diam. of lens,	4 x 4 in. plates,	3 in. equiv. focus,	each,	$25 00
No. 2,	1 " "	4 x 5 "	3½ "	"	"	"	25 00
No. 3,	1 " "	4½ x 7½ "	4¼ "	"	"	"	25 00
No. 4,	1 " "	5 x 8 "	5¼ "	"	"	"	25 00

---o---

Morrison's Rapid Stereoscopic Lenses

FOR INSTANTANEOUS VIEWS OR LAWN GROUPS

Are entirely different in many particulars from any other lenses in the market. They are 6 inches focus and 1¼ inch in diameter, and of course can be obtained in matched pairs, if desired. By using a set of diaphragms provided they are adapted for making 5 x 8 views.

A novel and ingenious instantaneous drop is also provided, passing through the brasswork, on the same principle as a central stop, by which *absolutely instantaneous views*, 4 x 5 inches, may be made, sharp all over to the very edges, without being diaphragmed down.

PRICE ... ...each, $40 00

"Peerless" Quick Acting Stereoscopic Lenses,

FOR PORTRAITURE OR VIEWS.

We can also furnish the following, either single or in pairs :

The Lenses are especially designed for Stereoscopic Photography, and are so constructed that they will work well for interiors or exteriors.

They are particularly adapted for instantaneous work.

Diameter of Lenses, 1¼ inch ; focal length, 3½ inches.

By removing the back lens and substituting the front combination, a focal length of 5½ inches is obtained.

They are supplied with six Waterhouse diaphragms in morocco case.

Price, per pair............................ ....$25 00

Imitation Dallmeyer Lenses for Landscapes. Price, per pair......$17 00

ALL STYLES OF LENSES TO ORDER.

Photographic Amateur.

By J. TRAILL TAYLOR.

Price, Cloth Bound, 75 Cents.

Price, Illuminated Covers, 50 Cents.

A BOOK of REFERENCE

FOR THE

YOUNG PHOTOGRAPHER,

Either Professional or Amateur.

SCOVILL MFG. CO.,

419 & 421 Broome Street,

NEW YORK.